An Informal Christmas
by Heather Gray

an Informal Romance novella

in celebration of my Savior
in memory of my daughter
with pride in my son
with gratitude for my husband

And the King will answer them, "I assure you: Whatever you did for one of the least of these brothers of Mine, you did for Me."

Matthew 25:40

One

July

Rylie ran for the elevator. A man in a faded denim jacket stood inside with the back curve of his left shoulder facing her. He didn't acknowledge her high-speed sprint in his direction. Nor did he stop the two brushed steel panels from sliding closed between them.

She thought of pushing the button and forcing the doors to reopen. Honestly, though, did she want to get stuck in a metal box with a man who didn't care about basic courtesy toward his fellow mankind? Not likely. Rylie huffed out an exasperated breath as she started up the stairs. Three flights up. It could be worse.

With a shove to the door, she exited the stairwell and stood on a narrow landing with skylights above and a view of the hospital's lobby below. Ten steps to the left, and she broke through to the hallway-of-no-return. Nobody came up to this floor unless they worked in one of the three departments exiled here. The first door belonged to the chaplaincy. The second led to the main office for the hospital social workers. The third door, decorated with construction paper butterflies and cotton ball caterpillars, was home sweet home — Child Life.

"I can't believe how rude people have become!" Rylie vented about the man in the elevator as she stepped past the colorful decorations and into her domain. Suzie, the part-time department head who kept their ship running tighter than junior size spandex on a burly linebacker, wasn't at her desk. Their offices were anything but spacious, though, so she was likely still within hearing distance. After all, what was a good venting without someone to listen?

"I was running for the elevator, but the guy inside didn't even wait for me. He let the doors slide closed. Because obviously it wasn't big enough for two of us." She left out the part about his back being to her. Absolving him of guilt wasn't high on her priority list at the moment.

Suzie emerged from The Vault, a nether region of their office used for storage. She dusted her hands off and frowned at Rylie. "We have company." She waved at the man following behind her. "This is Mr. York. He brought several boxes of stuffed animals for our kids."

No way. Not... Lots of guys wore denim jackets, right? It couldn't be the same...

"Sorry about the elevator. I got wedged into position by my dolly. I thought I heard someone calling, but by the time I turned myself around, the doors were closed and I was on my way up here." His voice reminded her of a lemon tart, decadent smoothness with a sharp aftertaste. For some reason, she found herself tempted to savor the sound rather than pucker. Too bad her mind was already made up about him. He might have proven interesting.

Guilt gnawed at her middle. *Sorry, God. I'll be nicer once I catch up on my sleep.* She sighed. *Okay, now I'm making excuses.*

"Yeah, well, no worries." Rylie waved a hand dismissively and slipped past him to reach her desk.

Had there been a dolly in the elevator with him? She didn't remember seeing one, but her single-minded irritation at the world might have prevented her from noticing it. She couldn't worry about that now, though. One of her kids was scheduled to start chemo later in the day. Two were going down for CT scans. Yet another had bone cancer that had led to discussion of amputation. The potential amputee didn't seem to mind — he was still at the age where scars were to be boasted about and *prosthesis* meant something super-cool and possibly cybernetic. His parents, on the other hand, were pushing the outer edge of hysteria.

And then there was Makayla.

In and out of the hospital most of her life, she was sixteen and full of spirit. Confinement to the pediatric oncology unit didn't suit her in the least. Makayla never meant to make trouble, but she always somehow managed to end up smack dab in the middle of it. This time she'd started a petition for Fourth of July manicures. Now every girl in the unit wanted one. In red, white, and blue. The fourth was in three days. How was Rylie supposed to find time to search for patriotic nail polish on such short notice?

She ran her fingers through her stick-straight black hair and sighed. It would have to come out of her own pocket, too. Suzie had reminded her just last week. The Child Life budget was maxed out. They were dependent on donations at this point, and nobody had anticipated the whims of a sixteen-year-old girl well enough to donate red, white, and blue polish.

"Uh, Rylie, did you hear me?"

She looked up from her desk. Suzie stood there, her wide green eyes expectant.

"Sorry, Suz. My girls all want their nails decorated with the stars and stripes, and I need to figure out how to make it happen. What did you say?"

Suzie shook her head. "Polish isn't in the budget."

"I'll work something out."

The hulking form of Mr. York remained over Suzie's right shoulder. Not that he hulked exactly. His was the wiry build of an Olympic swimmer, and if forced to guess, Rylie would put him at a hair shy of six feet tall.

Suzie waved a hand in their guest's general direction. "Mr. York here is planning on making monthly deliveries to us. He'd like to be able to coordinate with someone so he's better informed about the needs of our patients. I hoped you could be his liaison. You know, keep him up to date, that sort of thing."

"Liaison? Isn't that your job?" Rylie regretted the words as soon as they passed her lips.

The middle-aged woman shook her head as a shadow dimmed her eyes. "I'm part-time since the cut backs, remember? My job is to keep this department running, but there isn't enough time in the schedule for me to handle everything that needs attention. If I don't start delegating, I'm going to lose my mind."

Suzie wasn't to blame. The hospital, not her, had decided Child Life needed only a part-time administrator. To run the entire department.

Rylie sighed.

Working at a children's hospital affiliated with a much larger adult hospital had tremendous benefits. Their patients had access to treatments and equipment that a smaller facility on its own wouldn't be able to provide. It had its share of drawbacks, too, though. One such drawback was money.

Decisions were made based on profit, and the adult hospital — with nearly four times as many beds — dominated the spreadsheet. As a result, the children's hospital found itself in an indefensible position whenever budget cuts were discussed. If the adult patients didn't demand a service, that service was deemed unnecessary.

Times were hard, and it was apparent nowhere more so than in this forgotten corner of the hospital where everybody worked themselves into exhaustion so the patients wouldn't feel the pinch of reduced budgets and staff.

"Very well. Give me a second, Mr. York." Rylie booted up her computer and sent a message out on the intranet that Child Life shared with Social Work and the Chaplaincy. *Need red, white, and blue nail polish for the girls in Oncology. Anybody have some?*

She counted to thirty, hoping for a return message. None came, so she shifted her attention to the man who now leaned against the wall opposite her cubicle, arms crossed. As she did so, she prepared to send her computer into hibernation. The mouse hovered over the *power down* icon as a beep reached her ears. Her fingers flew across the keyboard as she typed in the command to bring the intranet chat box to the front on her desktop.

Dollar store by my house had huge display earlier in week. I'll check on my way home this afternoon. How many bottles?

Bless her. Blossom, the retired CEO of a successful technology firm, had realized too late that she couldn't stand retirement. She now volunteered as a chaplain to fill her time. Per her choice, she worked with adults in her official duties, but off-the-unpaid-volunteer-clock she did whatever she could to help the children's hospital.

Two of each ought to do it. THANK YOU.

She hoped those girls realized they wouldn't be getting flags and fireworks on their nails. Her skills were limited. It would be a good day if she remembered to paint one nail red, the one after that white, and the next one blue. If they were smart, the girls would give each other manicures and leave her, at best artistically challenged, out of the fun altogether.

"Ah-hem." The man still leaning against the wall cleared his throat.

A quick glance at the clock told Rylie she needed to be on her way. The first of the CT scans was scheduled to start in fifteen minutes. Scotty, an eight-year-old patient, had asked her to accompany him because his parents were at work, and he didn't want to be alone.

"Walk with me, Mr. York." She brushed past him hoping her voice hadn't sounded as cold to his ears as it had to hers. It wasn't his fault she'd been running nonstop since coming through the hospital doors hours prior — or that the day's race was far from over.

A second later, the yell came from behind her. "Watch out!"

Rylie spun around in time to see a previously stacked column of boxes tumbling in her direction.

Of course. The boxes with the marbles in them. Who had piled those blasted boxes so high? No one in touch with their sanity would be foolish enough to… Oh yeah. She'd done it. Because they'd needed the room.

A speedy jump saved her from most of the trauma, but the edge of one box landed on her left foot. Her yell filled their small office. Meanwhile, one of the other boxes broke open. Marbles began rolling across the floor. Rylie, her lost balance tossing her in that direction anyway, managed to throw herself in front of the door as she fell. At least the glass-orbs-of-doom wouldn't wander out into the hallway and cause further catastrophe.

Whose brilliant idea was it to donate a hundred pounds of marbles to the Child Life department? Now she remembered. The international marble champion Rylie had convinced to visit the hospital and host a demonstration for the children one afternoon had been so moved by the experience that he'd donated thousands of choking hazards to them. The boxes had been stacked in the corner so long she'd almost forgotten about them. Until now.

"It's awfully narrow in here. I brushed against a box. Sorry." Mr. York held his hand out to help her up, but Rylie wasn't sure she wanted to move. Some falls – and crushed toes – deserved to be babied for a bit. The image of poor Scotty, afraid of the CT machine, popped into her head, though, and she couldn't ignore the outstretched hand.

The benevolent stranger and knocker-over-of-boxes started to speak again, but Rylie cut him off as she got to her feet. "I'm needed elsewhere. Walk with me, or it'll have to wait."

"Don't worry about the mess here, folks. I have nothing better to do with my time." Suzie's indignant muttering followed them all the way to the elevator.

"You should get your foot examined."

Being angry at him would be easier if his voice didn't make her think of sweet treats on hot summer days.

"A little boy is going for an NBD test, but he's terrified. My job is to make it bearable for him, even if that means limping all the way there and back."

"NBD?"

"No Big Deal. The kids classify any procedure not involving needles, saws, or drills as NBD." The children actually said needles or a scalpel. She'd thrown *saws* and *drills* into the equation to get under his skin. Looks like it worked. So why didn't she feel good about it?

"Oh."

Rylie took a deep breath as the elevator eased down another floor. The time had come to start acting her age. Or even half her age. She wasn't exactly getting off to a good start with this man.

She held out her hand. "I'm Rylie Durham, the Child Life Specialist assigned to the oncology unit."

His hand enveloped hers in a warm grasp. "Zach York. I'm… the guy who knocks over boxes, gets himself jammed into elevators, and…" He rolled his eyes. "And apparently forgets his dolly up in the Child Life office so he has to go back for it later."

It was a trial, but she afforded him a smile. "What brings you to us?"

His shrug was a study in nonchalance. "Another time, maybe." He pulled something from his wallet and held it out to her. "Here's my card. Drop me an email within the next day or two so I know how to get in touch with you. When I'm ready to order some items for next month, I'll contact you and find out what y'all need."

She took the card but doubted any communication between them would be as simple as he made it sound. This man had complication written all over him.

"Ignore my email at your own risk, Ms. Durham." His molasses eyes glinted with a hint of mischievousness. "Or you might find yourself with more marbles instead of whatever children in the hospital actually need."

The elevator *dinged*, and the doors opened smoothly near the entrance to Oncology. Rylie stepped out but couldn't stop herself from glancing back at him. "Are you coming?"

"Not today. I need to fetch my dolly." He pushed the button that would return him to the forgotten corner of the hospital, and the doors slid closed.

Hm. He wanted to help the kids, but he wasn't eager to see them. He was either uptight, emotionally detached, or she was reading too much into his actions.

Tempted as she was, she couldn't take time to psychoanalyze the handsome Zach York. A wheelchair rolled her way, accompanied by a nurse. "Scotty! Sorry I'm late. You won't believe this, but a tower of marbles fell on me."

The little boy giggled and pointed to the foot she was favoring. "Is that where it landed?"

"Of course it is. You know I'm the clumsiest person in the whole world, right?"

Two

Rylie stared at her pager. It couldn't be. Wasn't he supposed to contact her to ask what they needed before showing up unannounced?

The message from Suzie said otherwise. Zach York was in the Child Life office, and he'd brought another donation. *A bunch of stuff,* according to the pager's display.

How dare he? It was one thing for people who didn't understand the way their department worked, but this guy knew better. He'd witnessed the tumbling tower of marbles and their limited storage space.

The elevator *dinged* its way open, and Rylie stepped out onto the landing. She didn't, however, stop to enjoy the view or let the sun from the skylight wash over her face. Instead, she headed straight down the claustrophobic hallway and marched her way past the Chaplaincy and Social Work offices. The Child Life door sported dinosaurs and space aliens this month, courtesy of a surge in the old-enough-to-color boy population of the hospital.

"Is he still here?" Why waste time on good mornings?

Suzie tilted her head in the direction of the hallway, which meant the man in question was either packing their storeroom to within an inch of its life or waiting in her little cubicle of an office. "Mr. York, I need a word." She spat the words out loudly enough to be heard no matter where he lurked.

A hand snaked out and grabbed her arm as she passed Suzie's desk.

Rylie peered down into the older woman's eyes.

"Go easy on him. He means well, and he doesn't look so good. Do you know yet why he's donating?" Suzie's uplifted eyebrow said it all.

Rylie released a sigh and studied the light fixtures in the ceiling. *Father, I'm in a rotten mood. Please temper my tongue and fill me with kindness and patience for adults today, as well as for kids.*

Sleep had chosen not to visit her last night, and if the dark circles in the mirror that morning hadn't given it away, her foul disposition ought to. The parents of one of her patients had suffered a complete meltdown the night before. They'd even used the D-word. Divorce. A nurse had texted to tell her. The couple's six-year-old daughter, after witnessing the whole thing, became so distressed that sedation had been ordered.

The Child Life budget didn't allow for overnight workers, and since there was rarely ever a need, it was usually a nonissue. After all, the kids were supposed to be asleep. The nurses were fantastic and handled whatever came up during the night. This, unfortunately, was different. A fight like that wouldn't be forgotten by morning, not by the young girl who had witnessed it.

Rylie shook her head. An attitude adjustment was in order. She was angry at the parents for fighting and frustrated she hadn't been present to intervene. To the mom and dad, it was a disagreement — nothing more, nothing less. To their daughter, though, who'd been given far too much to deal with in her short life, it was one more thing piled on top of the plate of wretchedness she'd been served.

Suzie released her arm but wasn't ready to let her go yet. "I've known you a long time, Rylie, and I've never seen you to take a dislike to someone the way you have this guy. I've also never known you to be ungrateful about a single donation to the children of this hospital. What gives?"

The words were a sledgehammer to her middle. In through the nose, out through the mouth. Rylie focused on breathing to alleviate the pain.

Suzie was right.

Rylie was out of control, and she knew it. She'd been heading down that particular slippery slope for a while but thought she'd managed to hide it from everyone.

She didn't reply to Suzie's question. How could she? She wasn't entirely sure she knew the answer. Rylie had a job to do, though, and she would do it. If she was lucky, she'd be able to pull it off with a measure of grace, too. With another deep breath, she stepped away from Suzie's desk and around the barrier into her cubicle.

"You look hideous." Rylie clapped a hand over her mouth. She understood the difference between thinking something and speaking it. Didn't she? "Uh, I mean…"

He shook his head, the barest hint of a smile tugging at the corner of his mouth. "I've had better weeks. Suzie…" He hooked a thumb toward the front of the office but seemed too worn to work up much enthusiasm for the effort. "She told me to stick around and talk to you."

Rylie sat at her desk and considered the man. His eyes were a washed-out brown today instead of the intense shade she'd seen before. It was as if they, too, were tired – too tired to hold their color. The lines around his eyes, almost imperceptible the last time she'd seen him, were now grooves carved into his skin. His forehead bore creases that his now-shaggy blond hair attempted to conceal.

Lord, give me the words.

"So, uh, what did you bring us?"

He grimaced. "I was supposed to ask what you needed, but I ended up with a bunch of books, so I brought those. Most kids are heading back to school, but some of the ones here won't get to. I thought they might enjoy having something to read."

She nodded. "Okay. What kinds of books?"

He shrugged, his gaze darting away from her as he did. "All ages. From toddler up to young adult, stuff for boys and for girls. I included coloring books, too. I assume not all the parents can sit here and read. They have jobs just like the rest of us, or other kids at home."

Rylie offered a smile. "It's a lovely gift."

"But not what you need."

Some nervous habits were hard to extinguish. Rylie's hand snaked up and tugged at the hair draped across the nape of her neck. "Child Life works in the entire hospital. My assigned area is Pediatric Oncology, so the things I think are important might not apply in other parts of the hospital. For example, my kids are always in need of goofy hats. Hair bows are in demand, too. Our girls with hair wear them, and the ones who are losing their hair sometimes wrap their head in a scarf and put a bow on that. Younger boys like pajamas with super heroes on them. Teens prefer video games. Most of the rooms are equipped with game consoles."

Her words petered to a stop as she realized she was answering a question he hadn't asked.

Zach nodded and rubbed a hand across his face. "Look, I'm sorry I didn't check in. Some things came up, and here I am." His words might have cut had he not appeared so tired. As it was, they came across as sharp as the preschoolers' rounded safety scissors. "Talk to me about next month. What will you guys need in September? Tell me now so I can plan ahead."

She could recite almost by rote the contents of The Vault. They were running low on everything their kids customarily used and were out of nearly everything that would be called for if a specialty case came up. "Stuffed animals are always popular, and we have a perpetual shortage of anything interesting to boys. It's easy for most people to find items the girls appreciate. Boys are a different story. People don't think they're as fun to shop for, so they end up forgotten."

His head tipped down in a nod of sorts.

"Do you want to tell me what precipitated your involvement in what we do here?"

Panic flashed through his eyes. If he were one of her kids, she would say he was afraid to answer. Either because he didn't think she'd approve of his answer… or because he didn't think he could say the words without crying. He wasn't a kid, though. Adults were infinitely more complicated. They had years of hiding their feelings and pretending to be something they weren't.

She was about to change the subject as she started to shift some forms on her desk, but her hand slipped. The stack fluttered in disarray to the floor.

They were only papers, and papers weren't a problem. Until she leaned down to pick them up, that is. Mr. Zach York leaned down at the exact same time.

Crack.

Rylie rubbed her scalp and winced. The instant headache was a doozy. She didn't know whether to admire the gallant behavior that had prompted him to lean toward the papers, or to be irritated. Gallantry didn't annoy her. Pain, however, did.

"What'd you go and do that for?" His gruffly mumbled question didn't sound at all apologetic. Maybe his head smarted, too.

"Look, Mr. York, my kids need me, so I should get going. Touch base with me next month. If we need anything specific, I'll inform you. In the meantime, keep in mind what I said. As for the books, they'll all go to good use."

Rylie slipped out of her cubicle and got past Suzie's desk before she took a breath. Once the elevator doors closed behind her, she put a hand to her head and let the tears come. She wasn't used to getting knocked on the noggin, and that one had hurt more than most. There was a joke in there somewhere about him being hard-headed, but searching for the words only caused the ache to increase.

What would he think of her abrupt departure? She'd done a lousy job of making a good impression on the man, so his reaction would be anyone's guess. Regardless, letting him see her cry was at the bottom of her to-do list for the day.

The familiar *ding* heralded her arrival at the designated floor. She wiped at her tears as the doors parted. Rather than stepping out, though, she stared at the man standing just outside the elevator. "Mr. York?" He had to have flown down those stairs…

He crossed the threshold and hit the button to take them back up to the Child Life office. "I know you're needed, but at least let me apologize."

Zach held out a tissue to her, which she took.

"You didn't do anything wrong."

"You're crying."

"It hurt."

A quick nod brought his eyes to meet hers. "As long as that's what caused the tears and not something I said."

Was he for real? She'd been a jerk from day one, and he thought *he'd* said something? "I'm afraid you haven't caught me at my best. Ever. I'm not normally so temperamental."

"I thought maybe… My sister would… I mean…" Color crept up his neck.

"PMS, huh?"

His gaze bounced off hers and refused to return. "Um…"

She chuckled. His discomfort did wonders for her headache.

They reached the Child Life floor, and the doors opened. Zach finally let his scrutiny settle on her again, the embarrassment of a moment ago gone. "Are you sure you're okay?"

"Yeah, and thanks for coming in and bringing the books. I take full responsibility for us getting off on to such a rocky start, and I'm sorry."

He smiled then, and Rylie caught her first glimpse of who Zach York was underneath that reserved exterior. She couldn't help it. She liked what she saw.

"No worries." He rubbed his head. "I do, nevertheless, think I'll take the stairs to be on the safe side. We don't seem to do well in confined spaces." He tapped the button to take her back down. Then he stepped through the doors and offered her a mock salute as they again slid closed.

Elevators were becoming a thing with them.

By the time she arrived at the oncology unit, Rylie had wiped away all evidence of tears. It wasn't like her to cry over a bumped head, even if it had been painful. Her emotions were far too close to the surface today.

Who was she kidding? Today was no different than the day before, the week before, or the month before in that respect.

Rylie made a mental note to email Zach later and apologize again. *And maybe brush up on those Bible verses that talk about controlling one's tongue and being careful how you speak to others.* Poor Mr. York had gotten the worst of her, no doubt about it.

That, however, was a problem for another time.

Rylie pasted a happy smile on her face and headed to Manuelita's room. The young girl deserved some extra attention today, and Rylie planned to see that she got it.

"Hey sweetheart, how's the food this morning?"

Her dark eyes luminous, Manuelita peeked up from her untouched breakfast and burst into tears. "I want… I want… to go home…"

Rylie pushed the tray aside, sat down on the edge of the bed, and pulled the girl into a hug. "It's okay. Mommy and Daddy are worried about you and said some hurtful things to each other. You didn't do anything wrong."

"They'll like each other again… if I go home…"

As Manuelita choked her words out between sobs, Rylie prayed. *Dear God. Help her. Help this baby who's done nothing to deserve this. Help her.*

Far from her most eloquent prayer, it was all she had to offer. There were days when complex sentences were too much effort. God was intimately acquainted with Rylie's heart. Her pain, too. He also understood what Manuelita was going through. In fact, not even the outcome of her battle with cancer was a mystery to Him.

Sometimes Rylie wished she could peer into the future. Which child would survive, which one wouldn't? She could better prepare them for what was coming if she knew. That kind of knowledge, though, would be a crushing weight. She'd never keep her sanity if she was able to discern the fate of her kids in advance. She was left with little choice but to leave that particular burden resting squarely on God's shoulders, the only ones strong enough to bear it.

"It'll be okay, sweetheart."

Manuelita's sobs quieted, and Rylie thought about what she could say to the parents to help them repair the damage. Would they realize the pain they'd created for their daughter?

Movement drew Rylie's eyes to the door where Manuelita's parents stood, their eyes suspiciously moist. She nodded to them. Even if the tears weren't spilling over, they were a good sign. And the couple was there together. That mattered, too.

"Look, Manuelita. Someone's here to see you."

The little girl glanced towards the door then reached frantically for a tissue. Rylie handed her the box and waited while the girl wiped her face. Then she took the used tissues to the garbage bin. If she were to hazard a guess, she'd say sweet little Manuelita didn't want her mom and dad to know she

31

was upset because she was afraid they'd blame each other. Last night wasn't the first time the parents had exchanged words at the hospital, but it was, by all accounts, the most explosive.

Mrs. Vega stepped into the room and sat in the spot vacated by Rylie. She reached for Manuelita's hands and held them loosely. "Your papa and I are sorry about last night. We're worried about you. We try to keep our worry away from you, but sometimes it makes us say things we don't mean."

Mr. Vega pulled a chair close to the bed and rubbed his daughter's back. "We yelled and made a big scene, and we're sorry Mannie. Nobody's getting a divorce. We love each other, and we love you. We miss having you at home where we can tuck you in every night, and sometimes we miss you so much that we say dumb things. Like last night."

Manuelita's gaze moved back and forth between her parents as she sniffled. "I don't want to choose."

Her mother scooped her up from the bed and stood, holding her daughter in a hug. Then she held a hand out to her husband, and he enveloped both of them in his arms. "No need to choose, Mannie. We're all in this together. As a family."

Rylie leaned her forearms on the pew in front of her.

The hospital chapel was quiet, the relaxing gurgle of a small fountain to her left the only sound. Funny how something so basic to life — water — could show its strength in how it soothed.

Is that it, God? Have I been asking You for the wrong things?

Suzie's comment came back to Rylie. Though she'd tried to hide it, her struggles at work were apparently not as secret as she'd thought.

I don't understand why You let children die.

She was called to work with children. Rylie had no doubt about it. Brightening a child's life, or even just their day, brought her immeasurable joy. It fed her soul.

When did I stop looking to You to feed the hunger in my soul?

It wasn't anything she'd done on purpose. She thought she'd brought God with her into every hospital room, every MRI, and every diagnostic report. Yet somewhere along the way…

I started leaving You out in the hallway, didn't I?

Why? She'd committed her life to Christ ages ago, and she'd done her best to live each day for Him until…

Somewhere along the way, I stopped trusting You with the lives of my kids. You let too many of them die.

Wasn't the power of life and death in God's hands, though? Everyone's days were numbered, and He was the only one who could count them in advance. The children who died, though, what about them?

They should have had more days, God. Why did You cut their lives so short?

Rylie waited for an answer, but none came. A voice from heaven would have been nice. She wouldn't have minded a promise that God loved all the children and wanted the best for them, that heaven was a glorious place for them to be.

The fountain continued to whisper in the quiet room.

So that's how it's going to be? I'm supposed to explain to myself why I should continue to trust You?

After all, she knew the truth. Jesus invited everyone — including children — to come to Him, and He promised abundant life to those who accepted the invitation.

I still don't understand why life is what's right for some and death is what's right for others.

Was it death, though? Or was it the best life, life lived out millennia upon millennia in the presence of one's Savior? But the families left behind...

I give up. I won't try to figure it out anymore. My mind will spin out of control until I'm consumed with questions about what You're doing and why.

Who was she to question the heart or mind of God? His love was beyond anything she could comprehend, and His will was perfect whether she understood it or not. Dying was a part of living, and while she couldn't control the one, she could do something with the other.

Okay, God. I'll give it my best every day. I'll love those kids and do everything I can to make this easier for them. And when one of them...

Could she say it and mean it? Rylie's pulse raced, her palms grew clammy, and her stomach acted as if it was cliff-diving. She'd come this far, though. She couldn't quit now. Her peace of mind — and her ability to do her job — depended on her finishing what she'd started.

When one of them doesn't make it, I'll give You my tears. I'll let You be the comfort and strength You've always promised to be. I'll stop trying to handle it on my own. At least, I'll do my best. I won't always get it right, and I'm counting on You to be patient when the hurt gets so big that I forget to let You carry it.

Rylie sat back in the pew and looked toward the front of the chapel. A small glass cross sat off to the right. Light from a nearby window caught it, and a rainbow of color danced across the walls. Most people would have been reminded of God's promise to Noah, but that's not where Rylie's mind went. A Bible verse came to mind instead.

I have told you these things so that in Me you may have peace. You will have suffering in this world. Be courageous! I have conquered the world.

Rylie pondered the words of Jesus, letting them circle through her thoughts and remind her that peace doesn't come from the world around her.

MEEP, MEEP.

Her pager pierced the silence of the chapel, jarring Rylie from her contemplation.

A quick glance told her she was needed upstairs. A family was about to get some bad news, and the doctor wanted her to be there in case the child in question needed her.

Three

September

"Mind if I join you?" Blossom, the chaplain behind the Fourth of July nail polish, called out to Rylie.

"Sure."

Blossom settled into the other side of the cafeteria's booth. "I like what you did with your hair."

Rylie ran her fingers through her ebony pony tail. She hadn't done anything different with it. "Shampoo. I'll let you borrow it if you want."

"Ouch." The chaplain gave a mock wince. "What's with you?"

"Zach York is supposed to come in again today."

"York? He the book guy?"

Rylie nodded. "One and the same."

"Be sure and tell him how much the kids appreciate all those books he brought in. Reading material's not cheap. That had to be a couple thousand dollars' worth."

"Yeah, I'll tell him."

Blossom lifted an eyebrow. "So what is it with you and him anyway? You don't seem thrilled at the thought of seeing him again."

"I don't know." Rylie shrugged. "I'm sure he's a decent guy, but he always seems to bring out the worst in me."

"Huh."

Rylie ogled the other woman. "'Huh.' That's all you have to say?" Indifference wasn't Blossom's usual *modus operandi*.

The older woman bowed her head and prayed over her meal before glancing back up. "When a man brings out the worst in a woman, he's either going to end up in bed with her or in jail for trying to get into bed with her. Or he'll end up married to her sister. Do you have any sisters?"

"Nope. No sisters."

"Well then…you might want to watch out for this one."

Setting her folded napkin back down on the table, Rylie stared open-mouthed at the chaplain. "Seriously? Is that the best you can offer? I want to get him into bed?"

Blossom chuckled. "Oh, I have better, but I find it telling that you went directly to bed and skipped over the whole jail part."

Rylie leaned against the padded seatback.

The chaplain cut a piece of pineapple into fourths and ignored her.

How long had she known Blossom? Long enough to know better. "Alright, alright. I'm going to dump my tray and go play nice with Mr. York. Do me a favor and don't start naming our children. Jail's still not out of the question."

Blossom's chuckle followed her out of the cafeteria.

This time as Rylie dashed toward the elevator, a hand reached out to stop the doors from closing. She brushed through the still-open doors, a *thank you* on her lips. The words died a sudden death, though, as she caught sight of the thunderous face of Zach York.

Should she ask what was wrong or automatically assume her presence offended him in some horrific way? How ridiculous! What was the worst that could happen?

"Is everything okay?"

His gaze cut to her and flitted away before anything close to eye contact was made. "Everything's fine."

The clipped bite of his words said otherwise.

Rylie crossed her arms. He might be one of the kindest men in the world and generous to boot — even if the elevator was markedly empty of the boxes he normally toted with him — but she wasn't obligated to take his attitude without complaint. "If you'd rather reschedule this meeting, we can do that."

Under her breath, she added, "Whenever you think you'll be fit company."

Zach's stare touched on her again, still not quite making eye contact, but long enough that she glimpsed the raw pain there.

Rylie took a step back. She'd worked herself up into a dither, but without uttering a word, he robbed her of every ounce of irritation. Many of her kids had worn that same look at one time or another. How had she missed the signs?

"I'd rather get this over with today if you don't mind." His voice was still tight, but the surliness had seeped away.

The *ding* of the elevator filled the small space, offensive in its cheerfulness.

Rylie silently slipped through the brushed steel doors and made her way to the Child Life office whose door, by contrast, was full of bright colors. Today it was decorated with portraits different kids had made of their pets.

Seeing that door almost always put her in better spirits, and today was no different. She smiled at the crayon drawing of someone's imaginary purple pet kangaroo before she crossed the threshold into the office.

The sight of boxes stacked almost to the ceiling brought her to a screeching halt.

Zach, unprepared for her sudden stop, slammed into her back and sent her sprawling. Rylie threw her arms out to break her fall, but before she made contact with the scratchy taupe carpet, an arm snaked around her middle and pulled her back.

"I'm sorry." His breath, a tantalizing caress, carried the rumble of his voice. A tickle made its way down her spine. Yep. Definitely a tickle. No way was it a chill. She wasn't a chill-down-the-spine sort of woman.

As soon as Rylie's feet were back under her and she was steady on them, Zach released her.

She immediately missed the band of steel circling her midsection and the heat of his presence against her back. Which was even more unlike her than having chills race up and down her spine.

To hide her flustered unease, Rylie stepped away and ran her hands down her scrub-clad thighs, smoothing away the invisible creases. "Talk about adding a little excitement to life." Not that almost falling was exciting, but how else was she supposed to fill the silence? "Thank you for the boxes."

Zach gave a brief nod and tucked his hands into his pants pockets.

"If this was a wrestling match, you and I would be on one team. Communication would be on the other. And we'd be losing."

The corner of his mouth tilted up. "We might be better off with dart throwing. I've never been much good at wrestling."

Rylie chuckled. She couldn't help it. "So, since I bombed on the whole following-up-and-coordinating-with-you-thing, do you want to tell me what you brought us this month?"

"Bowling balls."

What? "Bowling balls?"

He shrugged. "I figured they're not a choking hazard the way marbles are."

His implacable face gave nothing away, but surely it was a jest. Rylie took a tentative step toward the first tower of boxes and regarded them with equal measures of curiosity and suspicion. Nobody would be foolish enough to stack bowling balls that high… would they?

Suzie bustled in from the hallway. "Oh good! Did Zach tell you all about the treats he's donating this month? We've got enough sock monkeys to make sure every child in residence gets one."

Rylie stared at the man in question. "You were joking?"

"I am occasionally capable of humor."

She answered him with an eye roll.

"Did I miss something?" Suzie surveyed them both with a look that said, *Don't mess with the guy who gives us toys for the kids.*

Zach's voice was scratchy. "I, uh, might have led her to believe the boxes held bowling balls."

Suzie laughed then, and she had the kind of laugh that filled a space so completely that nothing negative dared fight for survival in its presence. Rylie thought of it as her boss's super power. One laugh from her, and disagreements were settled, grudges forgotten, and joy restored.

"Come on." Zach tipped his head toward the door. "I know we need to meet, but can we take it to the cafeteria? I need lunch. Besides, this place is kind of claustrophobic with all those boxes stacked everywhere."

Suzie waved them out the door before Rylie decided whether or not she even wanted to go.

"So, sock monkeys, huh?"

Zach shrugged as he stuffed a steak fry into his mouth.

"The kids'll love them." Rylie took a sip of her soda before picking up the pen resting next to her notepad. "We will never turn away anything you bring, but Suzie wants me to see if we can coordinate the rest of the year. Any objections?"

Zach shook his head as another fry disappeared.

So, a man of few words… Or polite enough not to talk with his mouth full.

Rylie tried not to be distracted by the memory of his strong hands stopping her from wiping out on the office floor. "October is Halloween."

Another fry vanished.

"Because our children come from so many different backgrounds, we recognize all the major holidays, but we don't force anyone to participate."

A frown tugged his lips down. "What do you do for this one?"

"Well…" Rylie cringed, heat warming her cheeks. Halloween wasn't the best example of what Child Life did for the kids. "We provide candy for anyone who's allowed to eat sugar as long as their parents don't object. Kids who are out on the main floor sometimes dress up."

"That doesn't sound like much."

She shrugged. "It's complicated."

His mocha eyes narrowed. "Explain."

She did her best to shrug it off. "We're near the nation's capital. We treat people from all over the world — all different nationalities and faith traditions. Every year, some of our parents object to a Halloween celebration for religious reasons. Some Christian families object; others don't. Some Muslim families object; others don't. They're not the only ones, either. The topic became politically charged, and Child Life was eventually ordered to give up."

One corner of his mouth tilted up, but she couldn't tell whether it was in good humor or sarcasm. "And what about you? Do you object for religious reasons?"

How should she answer that? She was trained to be politically correct, but a direct question deserved a reply in kind. "I don't personally take part, but…" She searched for the words. How to explain herself in a way that didn't leave her sounding hypocritical? "Ninety percent of children — regardless of faith affiliation — look forward to Halloween for weeks, and my job is to make their time in the hospital as easy as possible. If that means helping them celebrate the day, then so be it. Besides, having a choice about Halloween — or any other holiday — isn't in my job description."

Zach polished off the last of his fries and took a long draw on his root beer. "How about a costume contest?"

Huh. Weren't they at the part where he was supposed to tell her what he thought of Halloween?

He ignored her silent question as his own train of thought picked up speed. "Each unit should have its own contest. You'll want judges to determine winners. We can give out trophies for best costume, funniest, strangest, most colorful. We can come up with a dozen different ones if we put our minds together."

Rylie chewed on her lower lip as she wrote down the suggested trophy titles. It didn't seem that Zach was all that interested in talking about himself.

She might as well pick up the new conversation thread and go with it. "We can call it the Northern Virginia Children's Hospital First Annual Costume Contest."

"Uh, that's a mouthful, but I get the point. Leave the H-word out altogether, and maybe there'll be fewer detractors."

"Not everyone can afford to go out and buy a costume." Rylie wrote dollar signs down on her notepad.

"Let me check with a wholesaler I found. They had a great price on the sock monkeys. I'll see if they have any deals on costumes. Kids are resourceful, though. I bet you'll find they come up with ideas based on what they remember being in their parents' garage or hall closet."

Her pen *tap-tap-tapped* on the pad of paper. "I'm sure you're right. Children are remarkably creative."

"I might also know where to get the trophies. You work on the list. Come up with at least a dozen award titles and email me. We'll put the unit, the date, and the trophy title on each one."

Rylie jotted down his instructions. Then she wrote the word *Judges* and circled it. "You should be a judge."

His eyebrows shot up and disappeared behind the in-need-of-a-trim blond hair.

"You should. Can you make yourself available that day?"

"I'll think about it."

This was the second time she'd tried to get him in the same room with some of the kids. He seemed just as determined as last time to find a way out of it.

What was his story?

Four

October

"I brought you something." Zach stood there watching her, a wary look on his face.

Rylie worked up what she thought was a good scowl. "And you couldn't call first?"

Her scowl must not have been very convincing, though. Zach laughed at her. "Yeah, about that…"

She pulled the top box from the stack he'd brought. "Definitely not bowling balls."

"Costumes. In case anyone can't come up with something. Or doesn't have the money. Whatever."

Rylie glanced through one of the boxes. He'd covered all the sizes with some to spare. "The kids will appreciate it."

"Join me for lunch?"

Rylie settled the boxes into The Vault before turning to look at him again. She was more physically attracted to this man than she'd been to anyone… ever. That made him dangerous. On the other hand, there had to be more to him than coffee-colored eyes and lean muscles.

There was only one way to find out for sure. "The cafeteria okay? I need to stay on the grounds."

Rylie watched as Zach ate most of a chicken strip in a single bite. "So, uh, what'd you have for breakfast?"

"A lot."

She shook her head and looked at her tray. A whole wheat turkey wrap, pickle, baked chips, and water. His chicken strips smelled better than they should.

Zach tapped the table between them. "So what did you do with her?"

"Who? Suzie?"

He shook his head. "No. The gal who used to answer to the name Rylie and seemed like she wanted to chase me out of the hospital every time I came in."

Double ouch. Rylie supposed she did have some apologizing to do. "I'm sorry about that."

He shook his head. "Don't worry about it. Just tell me what changed."

She took a bite of her pickle to stall for time. The problem was that a person could only stall for one pickle bite. If she took two bites, she'd look like one of those people who bought whole pickles out of giant glass jars at convenience stores in rural towns nobody'd ever heard of.

"Are you going to stare at your pickle the whole time or take another bite?"

"I don't buy pickles out of jars." *Come on, floor. Open up. Swallow me. Do something!*

"Uh, okay."

Rylie reached for her water. "What was it you asked?"

Zach ate another fry. "If you were going to take another bite of your pickle. But before that, I asked what changed to make you so nice. A little odd, sure, but nicer than before."

She'd gone from a surly shrew to odd but nice. Was that an improvement? She couldn't tell.

"I work with a lot of sick kids, and sometimes those kids don't do as well as I'd like."

"And that makes you angry?" His voice held curiosity, not judgment. That was a good start.

"It makes me sad, but I wasn't handling it the right way, and it was turning into bitterness."

His gaze flitted away as a heavy blanket settled over the light banter they'd been sharing. "So what's the right way to handle it, then?"

He looked at her, a brief touch of his eyes on hers, before staring down at his tray. In that tiny little space of time, Rylie saw the truth. The question he asked was deeper and broader than he allowed it to sound. Whatever secret he kept, the pain of it was unraveling the fabric of who he was, of how he saw himself.

"I suppose the right way to handle it is to accept that you can't."

A derisive snort met her words. "What good does that do?"

She wanted to reach out, to touch the back of his hand where it clenched the edge of the table, but she held back. He needed to hear her words. They mattered more than any physical comfort she could give him.

Rylie swallowed her indecision. She drew on her training, the part that helped her explain the hard truths of a child's diagnosis. A real answer, no matter how difficult, was better than no answer at all.

"If you don't accept how weak you are, you'll never step aside and let God take the reins. In my experience, He's the only one who can handle the sadness and pain without crumbling under the weight of it. When we accept that we aren't strong enough in our own power, we give Him control, and everything we do from that point on is in His power. He has enough to go around."

Zach released his death grip on the table, but he still wouldn't make eye contact. Their light banter from before wouldn't be making a return appearance anytime soon. She could live with that. She'd said what she needed to say.

Rylie stood with her tray. "I wasn't trying to be preachy. And to be honest, it's something I'm still working on myself."

He nodded.

She rested a hand on his shoulder. "I hope the rest of your day goes well. I'll see you later."

Zach's phone rang, and Rylie took the opportunity to make her exit and save him from having to form a reply to everything she'd said.

When she reached the cafeteria's exit, she looked back at him. He sat there, his phone in hand but not at his ear.

Oh well. Maybe he didn't know what to say to that person either.

Rylie had been telling parents, nurses, and their young patients about the contest for weeks. The kids were exuberant in their chatter about the impending event. They would meet in the hallway and talk about what they were going to wear. Or hide away in their rooms and draw costume plans so detailed they put most fashion designers to shame. Even those who were scheduled for discharge before the big day got in on the fun by giving costume advice to anyone who would listen.

Suzie, ever the valued asset, had gathered judges. One was an off-duty pediatric ER doctor who'd promised to wear a rainbow wig and red clown nose. The mayor of Falls Church was coming as a firefighter. Before jumping headfirst into a political career, he'd been a firefighter, so his outfit ought to be easy to come by. Then, of course, there was Zach.

According to Suzie, she'd called him while he was at lunch with Rylie the week before but had been sent straight to voicemail. Hers was probably the call he'd gotten as Riley had left. Suzie thought of it as a coup. There'd been no need to convince their philanthropist to be a judge. She'd left a message telling him when to show up and to come in costume.

Now the day was upon them, and Rylie was scrambling to make sure everything went smoothly. She was thankful to be kept busy enough that she didn't have time to worry how Zach would act and if she'd said too much at that lunch.

They would start with the largest group of patients, the ones on the main floor. The kids were divided up by age, ten and under in one category and everyone else in the other. From there, they would head to the Intermediate Care unit to judge their costumes, then on to Intensive Care, wrapping up in Oncology. The Oncology kids were hers, and she couldn't think of a better way to conclude the day's festivities.

It was half past eight. The judges should be assembling in the lobby. Trophies were on their way to the nurses' stations in each unit where they were being kept under guard, literally. A couple of the hospital's off-duty security personnel volunteered to come in and make a big show of keeping sentry over the trophies.

The guards were in full uniform and determined to do their best impression of the British Royal Guard – stiff posture and blank expressions all day long. She wasn't convinced they'd be able to pull it off. The kids were determined to force a reaction.

"Places, everyone!" Rylie's raised voice carried down the hallway as the young patients from the main floor fell into line, backs straight, hands at their sides, doing their best to please. Bumble bees, princesses, warriors, and…

"Are you supposed to be toilet paper?" The boy nodded excitedly, his head barely sticking up through the brown cardboard tube at the center of his costume. Sure enough, he was a giant roll of toilet paper. *A future proctologist…*

Not all the kids were well enough to participate. The nurses wheeled out anyone who wanted to watch the contest. Even if they weren't in costume with the other kids, seeing the fun would brighten their day and give them something to talk about with the medical personnel who came in and out of their rooms all day long. As far as Rylie was concerned, the entire day was a win for all the young patients.

The judges walked up and down the line, chatting with the kids as they marked up their score sheets.

Zach was a cowboy. He sported worn leather chaps, a lasso at his side, workman's gloves, and a cowboy hat. Of course, he needed to remove the gloves to use his pen and record scores for the costumes, but the way he tugged them off with his teeth then tucked them into the back pocket of his jeans only served to make him that much more ruggedly attractive.

He'd greeted her with a quick smile and tip of his hat. Time alone was in short supply, but he didn't seem to be avoiding her. She would take that as a good sign.

Rylie hoped that, before the day came to a close, she would better understand the man who had shown up one day to bring toys for the kids and kept coming back. Zach York was a puzzle, and she'd never met a puzzle she couldn't solve. Until now. So far, whenever she'd asked him questions, Zach had turned the conversation back around and gotten her to reveal more about herself than she learned about him.

Once judging of the younger patients was complete, the older ones were called to order. Very few stood with the eagerness of the prior group. Instead, they slouched, tucked hands into pockets, and did their best to act as if they didn't care. They were zombies, vampire queens, hunters, the obligatory Uncle Sam, a sparkling piñata, and more.

Rylie raised an eyebrow at the piñata. The girl, eyes sparkling, implored, "Please don't hit me with a broomstick."

Rylie set the judges loose and stepped back. The ER doctor was fantastic in her nontraditional clown costume. She wore heels so high they threatened to cause a nosebleed and a fuchsia dress guaranteed to grab onlooker attention with its latex shine. Not ready to stop there, she'd added lime green tights, a bright blue bolero, an oversized red nose, and the curliest rainbow wig on either side of the Prime Meridian. She took the time to talk to each of the kids, too, and even visited with those not participating in the contest. She was a good person, and if the stories about her were true, an even better ER doctor.

The judging done, Rylie was given the pleasure of announcing the winners. Following Zach's instructions, she'd come up with a lengthy and creative list of trophy categories.

"This year's winner for Most Adorable in our children's division goes to… Suzie Metcalf and in our teen division… Leticia Velasquez!" The cute little bumble bee from earlier and a dainty fairy both came up to collect their trophies.

"Our winners for Most Original are… Georgie Whitehall and Samina Abdulla!" Toilet paper and a piñata trundled up to accept their trophies among cheers and whistles. A nurse sidled up to the one teen that seemed determined to cause trouble. The last thing they needed was someone throwing hurtful barbs at their resident toilet paper. Rylie admired Georgie's sense of humor. There would be no stopping him once he grew into his inner class clown a bit more.

"Next up, our Ugly But With Style trophy, and the winners are…"

The unit erupted in cheers as the judges excused themselves and headed on to their next destination – Intermediate Care. These were the kids who needed more attention than average but weren't in need of intensive care and didn't belong in Oncology. Some of them suffered from respiratory issues — severe asthma, viral bronchiolitis, or something similar. Others had the types of illnesses that, as a rule, would see them admitted to the regular wing of the hospital, but because of compounding conditions such as muscular dystrophy or cerebral palsy, they required extra oversight and ended up in intermediate care.

With fewer children in this unit, the judging would be done together with no age division. The kids lined up, but the atmosphere was quieter. Zach, walking bow-legged like a man whose entire life had passed with him firmly planted on the back of a horse, stepped over to Rylie and stood by her side.

"I wasn't expecting anyone in a wheelchair." His demeanor gave nothing away, but a person would have to be deaf to miss the strain in his whispered words.

"Ignore the chairs. Look at the kids and their costumes." Wheelchairs weren't inherently bad, but if he wasn't used to being around them, that's where his eyes would go. Children who depended on a wheelchair for mobility had a few pet peeves. People seeing the chair instead of them was near the top of the list.

"I'm not an idiot. I just wasn't prepared."

His words held enough of a bite that Rylie was tempted to glance down at herself and make sure she wasn't bleeding.

"It takes time to get used to the equipment. You'll adapt, but in the meantime, fake it for their sakes." She was proud of herself for not biting back.

Rylie sighed. There was a reason she'd dedicated her life to working with children. They were more understanding, sure. They also tended to be more forgiving than adults. And they hadn't yet learned to take insult at every little word.

Zach stalked off. At least, that's what she thought. To the casual observer, his walk probably resembled the lazy stroll of a saddle-sore cowboy.

If wheelchairs were hard for him, he might not survive the PICU. The schedule wouldn't allow for any dwelling, though, so Rylie shook her head and gave her full attention to the children.

Intermediate Care housed ten beds, all of which were occupied at present. Every patient was dressed for the occasion with the wheelchair kids decked out in spectacular fashion. A costume told a lot about how used to the wheelchair a family was. One wheelchair had been transformed into a blue police box, the child its famous occupant. The other was a bathtub with different-sized Styrofoam balls glued together to make the bubbles, its swimsuit-clad occupant sporting a grin.

There was also a pirate, a surgeon, a red plastic drinking cup, two princesses, a spider, another zombie, and the requisite cartoon character.

"Howdy, pardner."

Among all the sounds in the unit, Zach's voice was the one that reached Rylie's ears. He went down the line and interacted with the kids, even suggesting the zombie find himself a good hoedown. If he remained uncomfortable with the wheelchairs, he hid it well.

The Pediatric Intensive Care Unit was different from all the other units. Each of the judges, along with Rylie, was required to scrub in at the sink. They went room-to-room to judge the costumes of those who were dressed up. Sixteen of the twenty beds were occupied, but only three of those patients were in costume. In many cases, the children weren't aware enough of their surroundings to participate, and the parents were too overwhelmed to do anything about it.

The PICU was destined to be the most difficult of the units. She'd given the judges a brief talk about what to expect, but even so, the mayor blanched as they passed a room where a toddler was hooked up to a respirator, a feeding tube, and an external ventricular drain. He didn't voice the thought, but his face, void of color, screamed it. *No one so little should have that many tubes coming and going from their body.* He managed to pull on his politician's face and nod sagely to the weary parents, but the effort cost him, evidenced by the bleak eyes and drooping shoulders that appeared as soon as the door to that room was behind him.

They judged a pumpkin, a building block, and a hobo. The nurses and other staff filed into the rooms and clapped for each patient as they received their trophies.

Their time in Intensive Care was brief. Rylie was soon herding the judges toward Oncology.

She'd been looking forward to this all day. If she knew her kids as well as she thought she did, the judges were in for a surprise.

She hoped Zach and the mayor could handle the unique challenges of the upcoming group. The equipment in PICU was hard to get used to, but most of those kids would recover in due course and leave the hospital. Hers, on the other hand...

This wasn't the time to tell her judges that more than twenty percent of her kids would be dead within five years. Or that, among those who survived, sixty percent would suffer a chronic illness. Nor would she explain that the life-saving cancer treatments the young patients underwent would cause life-threatening side effects in twenty-five percent of the survivors.

She would give the judges a minute to shake off the aftermath of being in PICU before taking them to her unit. Meanwhile, she reminded herself that every day her kids were given a chance to act their age was a day worth celebrating. When she thought about it that way, putting on her happy face became an easy task.

Five

The costumed kids ran up to Rylie, smiles ringing their faces. Everyone wanted a hug, and she was glad to oblige. The oncology unit housed twenty-four beds. Eighteen were currently occupied. They'd sent two kids home the week before. She'd attended a funeral, too, but she wouldn't dwell on that.

The kids lined up, a colorful canvas of creativity, without being told. All eighteen children were in attendance, though some of the younger ones had been chauffeured by their parents in one of the unit's push cars. One baby was present. He was outfitted as a Dalmatian and looked a bit like a wriggling puppy in his mom's arms.

The line of costumed patients continued to grow until Rylie made a production of counting. As she reached twenty-four, she tapped a finger on her chin and turned to Zach and the other judges.

"Either our children multiplied, or imposters are in our midst. It seems that we're going to be forced to figure out which of these youngsters belong in the hospital and which do not."

"Pin the tail on the cancer kid!" The booming voice of one of the teens filled the whole unit.

Rylie's job wasn't exclusive to the patients. She did her part to make sure their siblings were coping with the illness, too. Brothers and sisters had questions and often didn't know who to ask. They also harbored worries and fears. The importance of finding them ways to feel useful couldn't be overlooked. Today would be a good day to play a game designed to do exactly that.

She glanced at the judges. "Think you're up for it?"

The fireman mayor wasn't yet over the nervous twitch he'd developed while in the PICU. The clown doctor smiled with delight. The pasty-faced cowboy appeared to be in danger of hurling. Not ideal as judges went.

"Give us five minutes, everyone. Go ahead and line up side-by-side. I'm going to explain the rules of the game to the judges."

The kids began to shuffle into place as Rylie headed down the hallway toward the small refreshment room. She punched in the key code, allowed the judges to precede her, then stepped in after them and shut the door behind her.

Her hands on autopilot, she retrieved three clear plastic cups, filled them with ice, and poured lemon-lime soda into the first. She shoved it into Zach's hand. He took the drink, his eyes overflowing with misery.

Directing her question at the mayor, she asked, "What's your poison?"

"The same is fine."

As Rylie poured, the clown doctor reached behind her, opened the mini fridge, and pulled out a bottle of water. She offered a small salute before saying, "I'm good."

Rylie took a deep breath. "Kids who are on this unit tend to be here for a long time, or they come back often. Because of that, we get to know their brothers and sisters pretty well. We do our best to make the illness easier for both the child who's sick and for their siblings. A few years ago, one of our patients invented a game. He called it Pin the Tail on the Cancer Kid. All our kids loved it, and it became a tradition that's been passed down from one patient to another ever since."

"How does it work?" The mayor drained his soda and set his cup down on the counter with an audible thump. Rylie almost expected the two-fingered brush telling her he wanted more, but he refrained.

"The patients and their siblings all dress up alike, and you get to guess which one is the cancer kid. You need to understand that there is no right or wrong answer. This game is fun for the kids because they get to try to fool you. What kid doesn't enjoy pranking an adult?"

Zach continued to sip at his drink. "The staff around here knows these kids?"

Rylie nodded.

"So how often do they get to play this? Don't most people recognize who's sick?"

She cringed. She wasn't fond of the word *sick*. But then, neither had she been crazy about *cancer kid* until someone created a game that made the term synonymous with fun. "These guys delight in messing with the new residents that come in and out of the unit. Anytime there's a new nurse, too. Sometimes even technicians."

Everyone nodded. Thankfully, some of Zach's color had returned. He'd done a fair job of holding his own until they'd crossed the threshold into Oncology. As soon as they'd stepped through those doors, he'd gone from merely uncomfortable to downright green... and not a cowpoke kind of green, either. With each passing second in the refreshment room, though, he returned more to his old self. Hopefully he could maintain it for the rest of the day.

"Remember, this isn't about how well you guess which one has cancer. It's about how well they can hide it."

Rylie led her judges back to where the kids were gathered. A quick glance told her they were in position. First in line was a group of three firemen. Well, two firemen and one firewoman. One of the early rules they'd implemented was that, to make the game fair, the siblings had to dress alike. These three, with their helmets on, made a challenge of telling who had hair and who didn't.

The judges quickly went down the row, made their determinations on paper, and then came back to a central location. The kids without brothers or sisters hung back. They would step forward again during the actual costume contest.

"Alright, I need my firemen front and center." At the sound of Rylie's voice, the three costumed children advanced.

Rylie glanced at the ER doctor, who shook her head. "I actually know this one, so I'm going to abstain."

"Number three." The mayor indicated the boy whose helmet was now coyly tipped back enough to show a hint of baldness underneath.

Zach's eyes narrowed at the quick grin of the number three. "Hm. I was going to say three, but I think I'll go with two."

All three kids burst into giggles. "I told you Sally! They fall for it every time."

The little girl whose strawberry blond hair was in two braids grinned, showing dimples and a hole where a matching pair of teeth had recently vacated the premises. The boys, numbers two and three in the judging, swept off their helmets, baring their bald heads, while Sally first pulled off her helmet, then removed her wig. "I'm the cancer kid," she said with a slight whistle, "and you couldn't tell!"

The trio ran back to their parents, and the boys began tugging off the hot vinyl costumes.

Next they came across two adorable pigs, curly tails and all. The judges got it wrong again.

The next costumed duo was a tricky one. The patient had an IV and didn't want it to give him away, so the nurses had helped dress his twin brother up with all the proper accoutrements until he looked like he, too, was on an IV. The pair was outfitted as…

Rylie laughed at their ingenuity. Dressing up as cancer kids would have been too easy, so instead they were women in labor. Fake hair, fake bellies, and fake… She raised an eyebrow. Hospital gowns usually hid people's shape, but these two had given themselves visibly healthy endowments north of their pregnant midsections.

Next up came two Dalmatians – the baby from earlier and a matching toddler who clung to her mom's leg and regarded the four of them with big blue eyes. The judges were about to make their pronouncement when the mom's phone sounded an alarm. She blushed and excused herself, taking the baby with her. The toddler, who had at long last released her mom's leg, batted her eyes at them and whispered loudly, "Chemo pee," before chasing after her mom on chubby little legs covered in faux Dalmatian fur.

The clown doctor opened her mouth, but a nearby zombie – which was apparently the theme this year – piped up first. "Chemo pee burns your skin. Not a big deal at my age, but if you're in diapers, you can get scarred up real bad from it. Juju's parents put a sensor in his diaper. Whenever it gets wet, their phone alarms so they can change him."

Rylie couldn't help but grin at Zach. The day's festivities were over, and the kids had loved every minute of it. Except for a few moments when her non-medical-professional judges had struggled with being out of their depth, everything had gone smoothly. Now her cowboy judge helped to box up the last of the unused costumes in the Child Life office.

"If they'll fit, stick them in your storage closet and keep them for next year."

She winced. The Vault wasn't all that big, but she would find a way to make it work. "You made a difference to those kids today."

As was the standard, he shrugged.

"Are you at least glad you got to meet some of the patients? Your contributions matter…" Her words faded between them.

He blinked it away, but not before she saw the glint of pain in his eyes. Had he lost someone? All his actions – from the donations, to his usual avoidance of the kids, to his reaction upon first walking into Oncology…

The death of a child could explain his behavior. Most of the time, though, people talked about it. Whenever she asked what prompted the giving, a person would mention the child, say the gift was in his or her memory, that they wanted to honor the child's life. Something other than his tight-lipped reticence.

Zach redefined strong and silent.

The urge to reach out to him was too great to ignore.

Is that you, God? Or just my own attraction? Help!

"Hey, I know lunch was provided, but we put a lot of prep work into this event. I want to go unwind. What do you say to nachos?" She hoped she was doing the right thing. "There's this great little place that'll let you order next to nothing and stay for hours. As long as you leave a good tip."

His hands disappeared behind his back. The next thing she knew, he was tugging his leather work gloves on. "Saddle up, pardner."

Oh dear. She hoped the teenage schoolgirl giggle bubbling up inside wasn't reflected on her face. She'd never cared for westerns before, but he tempted her to pick one up at the bookstore.

For the sake of professionalism, she rolled her eyes and shook her head. "You sure you want to go in costume?" *Change your clothes, or I might be incapable of coherent conversation.*

Zach's eyes twinkled. Within seconds, he removed his gloves, chaps, and lasso. Flames scorched Rylie's cheeks as he started unbuttoning his shirt.

"If you want to strip, at least let us sell tickets. It'd make for a scintillating fundraiser." Blossom stood in the doorway, inspecting the two of them with raised eyebrows and the sort of appreciative gleam in her eyes that people didn't generally associate with a chaplain.

Rylie dropped her gaze. Blossom couldn't have come thirty seconds later?

She glanced back up in time to see the chaplain circling Zach. His flannel shirt was gone, and he now sported a perfectly ordinary charcoal grey t-shirt. He'd been wearing it underneath the entire time. So the whole unbuttoning thing... there had been no undressing going on after all. Oy. Logically, she'd recognized that fact, but her reaction at the sight of him reaching for that first button... Well, logic hadn't quite been in play.

"Tsk, tsk." Blossom circled Zach. "Next time, leave the t-shirt at home. We'll set up a stage in the lobby, and you can take your costume off there. I'm pretty sure we could fund Child Life and the

Chaplaincy for at least another year on the donations alone. Social Work, too, if we raffled off the chaps and cowboy hat. Don't you think so, Rylie?"

Shaking her head at the glint in her friend's eyes, Rylie countered. "It being a pediatric hospital and all, the powers-that-be might not approve." Before the chaplain could say another word, Rylie escaped down the short hallway to collect her purse and jacket. She needed to get Zach out of there before Blossom said something even more embarrassing. She might be a chaplain, but that woman possessed a mile-wide devilish streak.

Rylie returned to their miniscule foyer to find her cowboy philanthropist alone, a bemused expression on his face. "She's a chaplain?"

A chuckle slipped out. "Yeah, and she's fantastic. Unorthodox, but fantastic."

Picking up his cowboy gear, Zach gave another trademark shrug. "Okay then. Lead the way."

Six

"Mm, these are good. How'd you ever find this place?" Zach reached for another cheese-and-pepper-laden chip.

Montecito's was a little hole-in-the-wall restaurant familiar to those, like Rylie, who had lived in Northern Virginia their whole lives. The people who loved the place didn't want outsiders ruining the atmosphere, so it remained a closely guarded secret.

"Montecito's isn't a place people find." She took a long draw on her water.

"No kidding." For a man who'd eaten a full plate at lunch, he packed away those nachos like nobody's business. "What? Is it a state secret? Should you have blindfolded me before bringing me here?"

She snagged a chip of her own. "That might've been a little tough since you insisted on driving."

"I suppose I should be thankful you didn't tie me up and make me get into the trunk of my car."

Rylie lifted her hands, palm up, in surrender. "Hey, some secrets are worth protecting."

His brown eyes, made darker by the dim lighting, flitted away. "Yeah, I guess."

"So what's your secret?" She concentrated on dissecting a chunk of nachos with her fork then moving it to her own little plate.

"I'm an open book."

Rylie reached for the salsa bowl. Zach didn't seem to mind the jalapenos, but he ate his nachos *sans* salsa. Lightweight. "Uh-huh. You ever going to tell me why you started donating to Child Life?"

The shrug should annoy her, but it instead got sexier each time.

She blinked the thought away. "I'm protective of my kids, and that means I protect the Child Life Department, too. I prefer to know who we're doing business with."

"Is that what this is, then? A business lunch? Should I write it off on my taxes?"

Zach's words held a barb, but she couldn't let it go that easily. "We live in a political environment. Everything we say and do is hyper-analyzed. As we're constantly reminded, Child Life doesn't bring money into the hospital. Neither does the chaplaincy. Both departments have suffered budget cuts the last four years running. Soon the hospital won't even cover the cost of Child Life Specialists, and something I went to college for years to learn will become nothing more than a part-time volunteer gig."

His shoulders dropped the slightest bit. "Accepting donations from me shouldn't get you or your department in trouble."

She'd been honest in her explanation... for the most part. She'd been defensive, too, though, and that wouldn't do. Rylie might not know what he was hiding, but she knew it was something painful. If she could tread carefully on the job, why was it so hard out in the real world?

What do I do here, God? You taught me to be open with others — transparent even — but this is different.

No. It wasn't different. Not really. Rylie realized it as soon as she finished the thought.

She took another cleansing breath. "Okay, so what if I'm asking because I'm curious? As an individual, not as a hospital employee. And as for Child Life, I don't think it'll ever be cut. I was venting. Feel free to ignore what I said."

The corner of Zach's mouth quirked up, and Rylie savored the victory. A smile on his face was a rare sight. This whole transparency thing was paying off.

"Well, then, as an individual, I should tell you I'm a fairly private person."

Rylie blew out a breath. "Huh. Go figure. I don't think I could have guessed that."

She might've poured the sarcasm on a little thick. His hand, halfway to another chip, dropped back and fell out of sight.

Never one to give up, she tried to salvage the situation. "I'm not trying to dive into your inner psyche. I simply want to understand."

He waved a hand toward the nacho plate. "I give you credit. You picked a creative way to go about it. You can try to get me to open up anytime you want if this is how you always do it."

At least he wasn't looking at his watch and claiming an early evening meeting elsewhere as a means of escape. "Tell me what you do for a living."

The tiny quirk was back at the edge of his mouth. "Construction."

She rolled her eyes at his droll voice and single-word response. At last his humor was present and accounted for.

"Construction has a lot of subspecialties, doesn't it? What's your area of expertise?"

"Mostly building. I build things."

Rylie closed her eyes and leaned her head against the seatback, ready to give up. She'd been wrong to think he needed someone to talk to, and she'd been even more wrong to think she might be the person to meet that need. This was the last time she let a pair of leather chaps decide her fate for her.

Laughter cut into her internal rant, and she opened one eye to look at her dining companion.

"You asked for it. I couldn't help myself." Mirth danced in his eyes.

Rylie tugged on her raven hair, a nervous habit. "You win. Is there anything you want to ask me?"

"Why did you pick Child Life as a career? Isn't it hard? Emotionally draining? Are you seeing anyone? How do you handle a kid dying? Do you ever let the kids see you hurting, or do you hide it and always put on a smile for them?"

"I think that's the most you've ever said to me at one time."

"I'm a man of few words."

"Unless you're trying to redirect the spotlight."

"Maybe. Maybe not."

She gave in. Arguing wouldn't get her anywhere. "I majored in early childhood education at the start of college. I wanted to be an elementary school teacher, third grade. I was observing in a classroom one day, and I met this little girl who wore a bright pink bucket hat to hide her baldness. During lunch, all the other kids went to the cafeteria, but she stayed and ate in the classroom. I got the pleasure of keeping her company."

The memory was a living thing to Rylie. She could smell the chalk and construction paper, taste the tang of her apple, and hear the slight squeak of the girl's desk chair as she shifted in her seat.

"Her name was Luana, and she had leukemia. Chemo had made her bald, and even though the doctor had okayed her return to school, he'd instructed her parents to keep her away from community areas as much as possible. Her immune system was weak, and they tried to minimize the chance of her picking up a cold or other illness."

"Wasn't it dangerous for her to be in a classroom with kids who went to all those same common areas?"

Rylie couldn't keep the sad out of her smile. "The other students washed their hands and used antibacterial gel. All the surfaces in the room were wiped off several times a day, too. The teacher even stayed late to scrub everything down with a special soap after school. The kids and adults worked together to make it possible for her to be at school and spend time with others her age. They wanted to keep things normal for her as much as they could."

"What about bullies? Kids can be mean, and she didn't have hair."

Rylie tugged her bottom lip in between her teeth. "I was in Luana's classroom for two weeks, and I shared every lunch with her. We talked about a lot of different things, including bullies. The occasional mean kid at school didn't bother her. The kids in the hospital, however, broke her heart."

"She was one of them, wasn't she?"

"Sure, but her mom telecommuted, which meant she could be at the hospital whenever Luana was there. A lot of the kids saw their parents only on the weekend. Their entire world became their illness. Every conversation was with a hospital employee and was centered on their diagnosis. Luana said they had the saddest eyes and that, if she lived long enough to grow up, she wanted to make life better for those kids."

Zach sat back. "Those two weeks of observation changed the course of your whole life, didn't they?"

Rylie nodded. "And I've never regretted it for a minute."

"Did she... did she live long enough to do those things?"

"I met her when she was nine. I exchanged emails with her mom and stayed in touch. I would visit now and then and tell her about my classes and what I was learning. We would talk about programs that hospitals should offer and what sorts of things would cheer the kids up. Nail polish and hair bows were always on her list."

"But did she...?"

Rylie didn't often tell people about Luana. She couldn't, not without choking on the memories. "She died a month before my graduation. She was twelve." Moisture pooled, and she glanced skyward in an attempt to prevent the tears from spilling over.

"Here."

A quick glance told her Zach wasn't fooled. He held a clean napkin out to her. She took it, dabbed her eyes, and blew her nose. "Sorry. I try not to let it get to me, but..."

"You care, and that makes you good at your job. Those kids swarmed around you the second we stepped into the cancer unit. That, more than anything else, tells me what a difference you make in their lives."

Instead of delving into the deep, dark secrets of his life, she'd managed to bare her soul. Her fate was sealed. She was never going to make it as a spy. Good thing she hadn't planned on trying.

"You didn't answer one of my questions." His voice held an undertone of teasing.

She'd missed a whole lot more than one, but if her guess was correct, he was referring to...

A glint entered his eyes. "So, you seeing anyone?"

Seven

November

Rylie got home from work and booted up her computer. She'd given Zach her personal email, and he had said he'd be in touch. Reading too much into it would be foolhardy. Just like falling for a guy who wouldn't open up about himself.

She wasn't falling, though.

She had it under control.

Zach's name in her inbox brought a smile to Rylie's face.

Okay. Maybe it wasn't as under control as she thought.

> *Hey Rylie,*
>
> > *Thought I'd drop a note and say hi.*
> >
> > *You told me how you have to accept your own weakness before you can accept God's strength. You know, to cope with your job. What do you do when His strength isn't enough? Or when He lets you down?*

Rylie stared at the computer screen for what felt like hours before moving her mouse toward the *Reply* button.

> *Hi Zach,*

I hope you're doing well and keeping busy with all your constructy stuff. You know, building and whatnot.

As for your question, that's a hard one.

I can give you the pretty answer, or the honest one. I'm opting for honesty. I hope that's okay.

Yeah, there are times when I've felt like God has let me down. That's kind of what led to my own struggle with stepping aside and letting God be strong for me. It's not easy seeing kids you've grown to love fight so hard to live — and sometimes lose that fight.

I guess the difference is that even if I feel like God has let me down, in reality I know he hasn't. When what I feel doesn't match up with what the Bible says, I tend to trust the Bible more than my own feelings. At least, I try to. I don't always succeed. But that's what it comes down to for me. I might feel like God has let me down now and then, but what I feel isn't always what's true or right.

I hope that makes sense.

And I hope you're having a fantastic day full of building stuff. Or not

building stuff. Whatever you think of as
fantastic.
Yours,
Rylie

A couple days later, another email came. Then another. Most of Zach's questions had nothing to do with God. He asked about where she grew up, her favorite foods, where she liked to vacation. Each time, in his questions, Rylie got to see more of who the man was. He opened up and talked about why he preferred the mountains to the beach — readily available lumber in case it was ever needed — and why he would never again eat soup in public — three clumsy waiters in three weeks soured him on the whole soup thing — but he gave no hint about what caused the shadows in his eyes and prompted him to wonder how people got past feeling like God had disappointed them. Somehow, with each passing day, Rylie was more okay with that.

Zach would share when he was ready, and if he didn't, she still enjoyed getting to know him. She wasn't willing to give that up in order to pry for information.

Not yet, anyway.

York's here to see you.

Rylie had agreed to let Makayla give her a manicure, which meant she could read the message, but typing out a response wasn't a good idea at the moment.

"What do you think?" The teen's dare was not lost on her.

A glance down at her hands showed nails decorated with neon blue and green in an alternating pattern. No one would be able to accuse her of being dull, that was for sure.

"I love it."

Makayla grinned. "Sure. And I have a head full of red hair."

Today's wig was cotton candy pink. Yesterday's had been lemon yellow. Red would show up eventually.

Rylie had asked once about the teen's penchant for bright colors. The answer had surprised her.

"Sometimes life is dark. So I splash color around wherever I can. It makes other people smile, and that makes me happy."

Makayla had been battling her cancer off and on for most of her life. She'd celebrated remissions… and lamented recurrences. Her entire family hunted for colors on her behalf. From bright wigs to socks and everything in between. They filled her hospital room with color at every opportunity. Rylie still remembered the day Makayla's grandmother had shown up with a shopping bag full of bras. Every stripe of the rainbow and then some, and not a single pastel in the bunch.

The poor teen had blushed furiously as her grandmother, all smiles and grace, had suggested she model them.

The silver-haired fox had known exactly what she was doing.

Yes, Makayla was a girl blessed with a family that went out of its way to bring joy into her life, even if it was occasionally at their own expense. Or hers.

Rylie's attention went from her nails back to the pager.

"Someone's waiting in the Child Life offices for me."

"Hot cowboy?"

Rylie's eyebrow shot up. "What makes you think that?"

"You blush every time I ask about him, and you're blushing now. Has to be the hot cowboy."

"I haven't even seen him since last month." And she hadn't, technically. She wouldn't mention the emails. Nor would she remind the teen that November was still new enough that *last month* wasn't very far in the past.

"Oh come on. It's not like I think you're running upstairs to go have office sex or anything."

"Makayla!"

Rylie and Makayla swung toward the voice and found Mrs. Maskey standing in the doorway, her eyebrows attempting to take flight above her wide eyes.

"You will apologize this instant. That is no way to talk to someone."

Guilt plastered on her face thicker than paste foundation, the teen met Rylie's gaze. "You know I didn't mean…"

Rylie rested a hand on Makayla's arm. "I know, but I imagine your mom has a thing or two to say about appropriate discourse." Then she leaned in close and whispered, "If I were you, I'd listen. She wants to raise you to be a magnificent woman."

The teen's woe-is-me sigh said it all. She would listen to the lecture, but she thought it was pointless.

Rylie nodded to Makayla's mom on her way out the door. Mrs. Maskey believed that letting her daughter get away with something because of the cancer would mean she either didn't love her child enough to raise her well… or that she didn't believe her daughter would live to see adulthood and so the raising well didn't matter. As a result, Makayla never had an opportunity to get away with much. If a mother's determination could cure cancer, people would be bottling Mrs. Maskey's essence to treat kids all over the world. That woman exhibited more fight in one minute than most parents would need to reach for in their entire lives.

"What took you so long? I paged hours ago." Suzie's voice was distracted as she clacked away at her keyboard.

"I was in the middle of getting my nails painted down in Oncology. I thought Zach wasn't coming until four."

The man in question stepped out from Rylie's cubicle. "I had another meeting cancel, and traffic was clear. I told her I'd wait and not to page you, but she wouldn't listen."

Rylie chuckled. "Suzie has a mind of her own. A thick skull, too."

"Uh, hello? I'm right here." The Jill-of-all-trades department head never paused in her typing. Suzie was a skilled multi-tasker if ever there was one.

Zach came down the short hallway. "I wanted to talk about Thanksgiving, but I'd rather not be stuck in an office. Want to go sit outside?"

"Give me a sec." Rylie scooted past him to her cubicle and collected her notebook.

"All set?" His arms were crossed, his fingers drumming out a silent rhythm.

She gave him a nod. "Follow me. I know the perfect place."

The hospital grounds included two outdoor courtyards. She led him to the one located by the pediatric wing. How would he react to sitting in clear view of kids coming and going through hallways? She hadn't given up on figuring him out. A little observation might tell her what his emails had not.

Within a few short minutes, they were settling onto the benches of a picnic table. Rylie set her notebook down and flipped it open to a blank page. Should she say what was on her mind? "You look tired."

"Been working hard."

"I thought construction work was scarce during the cold weather."

Zach snorted. "Maybe in the rest of the country, but not in Northern Virginia."

"You should slow down then. You seem more worn out than usual."

If laughter could have fangs, his did. "You're not a nurse, okay? Leave it alone. Let's talk about Thanksgiving."

The whole conversation was out of character. Zach could get defensive when she probed, but this was different. He was different. And she had no idea how to respond.

"Fine. Did you have something in mind?"

He nodded. "I know a guy. He has a restaurant over at National Harbor. They flooded after the last hurricane, and I did some repair work for him. He owns other restaurants, too. I was thinking of asking him to cater a Thanksgiving dinner for the kids."

"That's a big expense. Include the families — which you pretty much have to do for the big holidays — and you're talking about catering for over five hundred people. Are you sure he's willing to do it pro bono?"

Zach shrugged. "Can't hurt to ask."

Rylie chewed on her lower lip.

"Spit it out. You've obviously got something on your mind."

Was it her, or was he in a mood? Where was the Zach she'd gotten to know via email?

This wasn't the time or place, though. She would let it go. "The cafeteria here does a decent job for Thanksgiving dinner. I'm sure they have deadlines, too. Let me talk to the guy who handles food service to see if they've already ordered a kazillion pounds of mashed potatoes."

"You do that, and I'll check with my guy." He stood to leave, but Rylie couldn't let him go yet.

"We're talking about a meal in less than two weeks. Lollygagging is out of the question."

He peered from the door leading into the building to her. His posture was stiff, the lines of his face hard. Shadows had gathered in those rich brown eyes that normally reminded her of steaming coffee. "Lollygagging? I think I heard my great-grandmother say that once."

Rylie opted not to defend her vocabulary to a man who was her age or close to it. Besides, the word wasn't archaic. Not exactly.

Zach took a step toward the door before glancing down at her. "Why don't you go check with the cafeteria people, and I'll call my guy."

She rose to her feet. "Sounds good. Meet me up in my office before you leave, though, so we can talk some more to figure out if this is going...?"

His head was shaking before she finished. "Let me take you out to dinner."

She raised an eyebrow.

He shoved his hands deep into his pockets. "You win. I don't want to be here today. I want to be anywhere but at the hospital, okay?" He said the words as though he intended for them to sting, but they somehow lacked venom.

"We can meet somewhere if you want. I get off around five, give or take."

Zach ran a hand over his face. "Montecito's? Six?"

She nodded before rising from the table and marching toward the door. Every fiber in her being called at her to stop, to go back to him, to find out what was wrong. The still, small voice, though, told her to let it go.

So she walked away when it was the last thing she wanted to do.

IGHT

Rylie sat in a circular corner booth and played with the drops of moisture forming on the outside of her water glass. The calendar said fall was moving on its way to winter with more speed than a just-fired human cannonball. There shouldn't be condensation, but the droplets on the smoky glass attested to the high humidity and unseasonably warm weather.

Zach slid into the booth. "We're getting more than nachos this time, just so you know."

"Abso-total-utely." She refrained from asking how he was. Her prying days were over, at least until the next time her curiosity got the better of her.

He was going through something, but it was apparent that he had no intention of sharing what was on his mind. Rylie's penchant for trying to fix things worked in her favor on the job, but it wasn't always an asset in her personal life.

"So what do you recommend here besides the nachos?"

"The *tres leche* and the flan. Both are divine."

He returned her grin. "So appetizers and dessert, huh? I like a girl who has her priorities, but let's pretend for a minute that I'm a man who needs actual sustenance. What's good?" He waved his hand at the menu sitting beside her placemat. "And don't you dare say *the salad*."

She liked this new and improved mood of his even if it did make her question her *I-will-not-pry* stance. "The fajitas are out of this world, but if you want all the flavor without the fuss, get the fajita burrito. You'll think you dived into a fajita lake, and coming up for air will be the last thing on your mind."

"Sold."

The waitress approached and took their orders. After she brought Zach's ice tea, she retreated and left them in peace.

Fighting a case of the fidgets, Rylie continued to toy with the condensation on her glass. "The head of cafeteria meal-planning gave me seventy-two hours to decide. He has to order his food a minimum of ten days in advance for Thanksgiving, and we're now at two weeks out."

Zach took a draw on his tea. "Miguel, the guy I told you about, owns four restaurants including the one at the National Harbor. They're high-end, the kind I can afford to work on but not eat at. He runs a charitable foundation that all his restaurants feed into. He can handle the catering and use the cost as a tax write-off, but he decided to let his customers dip into their pockets for the sake of philanthropy. People tend to be in more of a giving mood this time of year. At least, that's what he told me. Starting with this evening's dinner service, his wait staff will give each customer an opportunity to donate to the cause. He said he'd call me with an update in a day or two to tell me how much money's been raised, but that his foundation would cover anything the donations don't."

The nachos arrived, and Zach reached with his fork to disentangle a chunk. "He didn't explain the whole thing to me, but he did say everyone who contributes will get a tax deductible receipt. He's planning to send two people from each of his restaurants. They'll bring the food in, set it up, and do the breakdown and cleanup afterward. We'll have to provide the volunteers to serve." Before she could interject, he continued. "I'm pretty sure I can round up half a dozen. How many do you think we'll need?"

Rylie debated her next question. "And you're sure he's aboveboard?"

Zach shook his head dismissively. "I was already aware of the foundation, which is why I thought of him. I did my due diligence, though, and checked it out before making the suggestion. I couldn't find any bad reviews or watchdog alerts."

"Watchdog?"

"Yep. There are places that keep an eye on nonprofits and report any malfeasance, that sort of thing."

Huh. She hadn't seen that coming. She'd thought it more of a whim on his part when he first suggested it, and then he'd avoided addressing the legitimacy of the offer the first time she'd asked. Yet one more thing to put in the he's-a-mystery column.

Rylie pulled her mind back to the issue and ran through the figures in her head. "Between the restaurant people and your volunteers, that should be enough. Parents will pitch in if we end up shorthanded. They're good about that. So, uh, do I want to know how much this would cost if he weren't raising the money himself?"

A smile split Zach's face. "We need to get as close to an exact count as we can so he can plan the food preparation accordingly, but I told him to expect around five hundred. He said an event of this size would normally run over twenty thousand dollars."

Her sudden inhalation of breath lodged a chip in Rylie's throat.

Zach chuckled. "Don't worry. That price includes all the bells and whistles. Linens, wait staff, et cetera. Besides, he's not charging us, so it's a moot point."

If she ever got married, the reception would be pot-luck. No way would she pay for catering.

Two days later, Rylie received a brief email.

Miguel says we're good to go. Over $2000 raised in first day & a half. The headcount you gave me helped.

She sent a message back.

What if he doesn't raise all the money? Child Life can't afford to pay for this. Maybe I should call and talk to Miguel myself. Or you could ask again just to be sure?

Three deep cleansing breaths later a reply came. She hadn't even finished worrying about the problem yet.

The $20K was retail. At cost, it's a lot less. And I already double-checked. (I knew you'd ask.) No worries. Child Life won't owe anything.

Now stop worrying about it and tell me about your day.

Rylie exhaled.

Okay.

This was good.

And she knew how to delegate.

It wasn't like she had to run the event for all departments on Thanksgiving Day. Each of the Child Life Specialists could pitch in and get their areas organized so all she'd be required to do was direct the workers to their designated locations.

The PICU couldn't allow the caterers in because of their infection protocols, so their meal would be set up in the waiting room. The NICU decided they wanted in, too. Even though the babies couldn't eat, their families would need food. They would be sent to the PICU waiting room, as well, since the numbers for both those areas were relatively small.

This time, when she reached for the reply button, it was with a smile.

One of my kids threw up in the CT room. It wasn't a big deal, but the tech running the CT had a really strong gag reflex. Her job's on the line if she leaves the room with other people in there, so she had to stay while we cleaned everything up. It was too much for her. She ended up huddled in the corner with a garbage can. Poor woman. She's only been on the job two months. This was her first day flying solo without a trainer.

His reply came almost instantly.

I know I shouldn't have, but I laughed. Poor woman, sure, but poor kid, too. Throwing up's never fun.

My sister has a strong gag reflex. So does my mom. When I was growing up, anytime the dog made a mess — out of either end — one of them would throw a towel over it and wait until my dad or I came to the rescue to clean it up. We could handle it, but they sure couldn't.

Her picture of Zach York continued to develop like film in a tray of solution. More color and depth showed up with each passing second. Her fingers flew as she typed her response.

> *So, basically, you're the rescuer of damsels in stinky messy distress? I don't know whether to respect you for it or to take two steps away... After all, I don't want to be nearby the next time you're called on to clean something up. Maybe I'll just stand over here. By the window, so I can open it in case I need fresh air.*

She must be tired. It had sounded funny in her head, but once she clicked *send*, she wasn't so sure anymore. Oh well. It wasn't like she could call the email back. Or could she?

The computer *dinged* with an incoming message before she had a chance to figure out whether or not she could call her last one back.

> *Hey, tell me something. When you're having a hard time with God, do you still pray? You know, like when you feel He's disappointed you or something?*

Their conversation had just taken a sharp turn from clowning to serious. Rylie sent a quick prayer heavenward before typing out her answer, an answer that would require her to share her heart on the subject.

Promise not to laugh? Yeah, I still pray, but sometimes it's to tell God I'm not speaking to Him. Silly, right? I know He can see what's in my heart, so He already knows when I'm hurt or angry, but I still tell Him. When I stop talking, that's when those dark feelings fester. Keeping the communication open — even if it's to rant or tell Him I think He messed up —helps me to heal.

It's the same as with family, or even in marriage. Things happen, and people get upset. If nobody talks it through, those feelings grow until they become ugly and all-consuming. Talking helps keep the emotions in perspective.

Okay, it's not exactly the same. In marriage, it's two people, and people mess up. With me and God, I'm the only one who messes up. Still, you get the idea.

So, yeah, I still talk to Him, and sometimes I sound like a tantrum-throwing teenager, but I'm a work in progress, so I don't sweat it too much. As long as I'm trying to grow and do better, I figure that's the most important thing.

No reply came, but she didn't really expect one. Whenever Zach asked a serious question, that was usually the end of their back-and-forth email exchange for the day. She wasn't sure yet if it was because he wanted to mull over her answer or because he didn't like what she'd said. Either way, they were done.

Rylie shut down her computer and headed toward her small kitchen.

The leftover meatloaf in the fridge was calling her name.

Help him find his way, Lord, and protect my heart from getting more involved than is wise.

She had a feeling it was already too late for the latter...

Nine

A prolonged blast of frigid wind welcomed Thanksgiving Day. Leaves tumbled from nearby trees as Rylie's fingers, gloved against the biting cold, fumbled with her keys while struggling to hold a stack of file folders.

She made her way up to the Child Life office and through the handprint-turkey decorated door to drop everything onto her desk. The hollow *thud* echoed in her cubicle. What had she been thinking? She shouldn't have brought those files home the night before.

Whenever one of her kids was out of the hospital for a year, she did a follow-up check on them at home to see how they were doing. Not part of her job description, it was nonetheless encouraged. That was bureaucratic talk for *use your own time*.

Taking files home each month and making the handful of calls wasn't a bother. Oncology patients returned so frequently for additional treatment that whenever somebody went a whole year without coming in, it tended to mean good news. There wasn't much of a positive spin she could put on this month's calls, though. Thirty-two kids from her unit hadn't been admitted since the previous

November. Half a dozen of them had stopped in to say hi at some point when they'd been in the hospital for one thing or another, so she already knew their status. Of the remaining twenty-six, she had attended two funerals.

Seeing the names again and knowing those children hadn't survived was always hard, but it came with the job. She could deal with it, as long as she remembered to turn to God for strength. This month, however, as she'd phoned the families, she'd been informed of four additional deaths.

Idiocy. Making those calls on the eve of Thanksgiving had been pure idiocy on her part. Either her brain cells had vacated the premises, or she was a masochist. She preferred to think it was the former, not the latter. Regardless, she wouldn't make that mistake again. Which, now that she thought about it, plainly meant she wasn't a masochist. It didn't, however, make up for the fact that she'd given each of those families a vivid reminder of what — and who — they'd lost.

As somber as the day would be for her in light of the sad news absorbed the night before, she personally knew several families who would all be experiencing their first Thanksgiving without a beloved child. She shoved the thought down deep inside and did her best to seal off the weeping emotions. People expected a celebration today, and she would give them one. The gloomy weight of grief would still be lurking around later if she decided to spend some time with it.

"Hey. Everything okay?" Zach stood there, concern etched into the lines and curves of his face.

"Yeah." She began unwinding her scarf.

He moved closer and held something out to her. Rylie forced herself to focus on the item in his hand.

A box of tissue.

"You're crying."

She reached up to feel her face, but rather than feel tears on her fingertips, she felt cold leather against her cheeks. Her gloves were still on. Shaking her head in denial, she pulled a tissue from the box and wiped off her cheeks. "Sorry. I'm not sure what came over me."

"What's wrong?" His voice whispered through the air.

The irony wasn't lost on her. The man who couldn't tell her a single thing about himself wanted her to bare her heart. Uh-uh. Not going to happen. She would take time to sort through her emotions and face each one later. For now, compartmentalization was the order of the day.

"Nothing I can't handle. When do your volunteers arrive?"

His face tightened and his eyes narrowed as though he was digging in for an argument. He glanced over his shoulder, though, and Rylie realized they weren't alone. The small foyer overflowed with people displaying happy holiday grins, and she wasn't beyond exploiting their presence to save her from having to explain herself.

Rylie did what any reasonable adult would do. She walked past the man standing in the entry to her cubicle without acknowledging him and went to welcome his entourage.

He'd either decide she was angry… or blame PMS. The truth was, if she looked into his eyes one more time, she'd lose the small bit of her self-control that still remained. If that happened, there wouldn't be any way to get the tears — or her emotions — back under control. She couldn't even risk explaining.

I could use a break here, God. Don't let me drive away someone who's trying to help.

"Thank you all for coming. I'm Rylie Durham, and we're going to have a fantastic day. If everything goes according to plan, you'll be out of here in time to go home and enjoy your own Thanksgiving dinners."

A man with a sturdy build, tanned skin, and a fair amount of salt and pepper in his brown hair held out his hand. "My name's Peter York, and this is my wife Abigail." He indicated the smiling woman at his side.

Wait a minute… "York?"

Abigail grinned. "Didn't Zach tell you he was bringing the family? That boy of mine can be as stingy with his words as a miser with his money."

"I'm standing right here, Mom." Zach's exasperation spoke to a long-running joke.

Peter circled toward an elderly couple to his left. "These are my parents, Tom and Bertha York."

"It's nice to meet you both. You must be very proud of Zach for working so hard to help the children in our hospital." Rylie shook their hands but didn't miss the look all six people exchanged. Without uttering a word, they'd communicated something about the mysterious philanthropist who had shown up in her office all those months ago. Too bad she didn't speak their silent language.

She pivoted toward the last couple and waited to be introduced. Peter didn't waste time. "Back here is my brother Sam and his wife Cleo. It's short for Cleopatra, but she's not quick to forgive anybody who calls her by her full name, so stick with Cleo."

The woman in question swatted Peter on the arm before shaking Rylie's hand.

"So this is a York family reunion then? If I'd realized, I'd have made a sign."

Abigail smiled. "Not our whole family, but enough to make today a grand success."

Zach had inherited his mother's eyes. It wasn't merely the deep chocolate color, either. Despite their smiles, the same sadness lurked in both.

Rylie clapped her hands and rubbed her palms together. She finally had access to answers about Zach. Of course, she had no intentions of prying. For the most part. It was like receiving a bowl of ice cream while being told she was lactose intolerant.

A light tap at the door drew her eyes. "Mom! You made good time."

Jessica Durham stood in the doorway. Rylie knew what everybody else would see. Aside from a few lines and a smattering of grey here and there, she and her mom could pass for sisters. They had the same pale skin, green eyes, and straight black hair.

"This is Thanksgiving, dear." The southern lilt to Jessica's voice never lost its charm. "The only people on the road are the husbands who forgot to stop by the store and buy a turkey like their wives told them."

After taking everyone on a quick tour of the different areas and explaining how their stations would be set up, Rylie assigned volunteers. Thankfully, Blossom and another chaplain stopped in to lend assistance, too. With the added influx of families from the NICU, those extra hands were more than welcome.

Zach's aunt and uncle and grandparents were sent to the main floor. Blossom and the other Mr. and Mrs. York — Zach's parents — handled the PICU and NICU crowds. Jessica and the other chaplain took the Intermediate Care Unit, which left Rylie and Zach in Oncology.

Hours later, Rylie was in the midst of dishing up what must have been her fiftieth piece of pumpkin pie to a waiting plate — a plate already filled twice before — when a hand on her shoulder drew her attention. Abigail stood at her side.

"Is the PICU finished? That was fast." Rylie scooped whipped cream onto the pie as she examined the woman whose grey hair was freed from the obligatory net that still captured her own and scratched at her neck.

Abigail shrugged and resembled her son even more. "The diners in our area came and went pretty quickly. People collected their food then returned to their units. Nobody was inclined to stick around and socialize."

Rylie was about to ask if the caterers had left yet, but Abigail's soft voice stopped her.

"I want to thank you for all you've done to help Zach."

What was she talking about? "It's the other way around. He's helped us."

Abigail shook her head and cast a furtive glance over Rylie's shoulder. "His baby sister moved

111

overseas with her husband and daughter. Our son-in-law's company transferred him to Japan for two years. As soon as they got settled, Cassidy got sick."

"Your daughter?"

Abigail shook her head. "Granddaughter."

Ah... That explained a lot. "Zach's niece."

The older woman nodded sagely. "Cancer."

Rylie resisted the urge to ask how the girl was. For all she knew, this was their first Thanksgiving without Cassidy. The last thing she wanted to do was prod those still-raw emotions in such a public place.

"We're all so far away, and there's nothing we can do. Zach took it the hardest." A heavy weight in her words, Abigail added, "He's the most doting uncle you'll ever meet, and he's used to doing things. He prefers to fix problems rather than watch them. Not being able to do anything was crushing him."

The movement surrounding them slowed. Sounds became muffled. Colors bled into each other until they blurred. Rylie blinked. She stared directly at Abigail, but all she saw was a memory of pain flashing in Zach's eyes. Then suddenly, like an airplane taking off, everything sped up. Colors separated themselves out and sounds once again grew distinct, and in that moment, everything about him that hadn't made sense became clear. It was as if someone had played with the sharpness setting on a computer monitor and brought it all into crisp focus.

"And that's what brought him to us." Rylie's words came out in a whisper.

If a smile were capable of weeping, it would look like Abigail's in that moment. "Cassidy's a bright cookie. He asked her what he could do to help, and she suggested he find a local children's hospital and do something for the kids there. So he did, and he's brought her along for the journey. They talk every week. He lets her pick what to buy. She told him there weren't enough stuffed animals at her hospital, so he bought you stuffed animals. Cassidy told him they needed more books, and he shopped for books. Our poor girl was sad about missing Thanksgiving dinner because it's Japan and her hospital won't be serving turkey and stuffing, so her uncle went out of his way to pull this together for the kids here."

Questions whirred in Rylie's mind, but Zach was approaching them, suspicion on his face.

Abigail squeezed her hand. "Regardless of whether or not you knew you were helping him, I wanted to say thank you."

The older woman turned to the next person in line. "Pumpkin or pecan? I think there might be apple, too."

Laughter at the unit's entrance drew Rylie's eyes. Her mom stood with Blossom, Peter, and Zach's grandparents. They must be done over in Intermediate Care, too.

All that remained were the main floor and Oncology, where things were steadily winding down.

Another glance revealed her mom heading in her direction, determination in her step. Oh dear. The last thing she wanted was an inquisition about the handsome philanthropist. She might have mentioned him a time or two. Or three.

Abigail abandoned the pie station and intercepted Rylie's mom. Saved! Then reality set in. Her mom chatting with his mom? That couldn't be good.

Zach cast a thin-lipped frown in the women's direction.

Rylie needed to get them all out of there, and sooner would be better than later. "I'd say we're about done here. What do you guys think?" Her question wasn't directed at anyone in particular, but the two restaurant employees both nodded. They'd each mentioned having family plans for the afternoon.

She yanked her hair net off, freeing her dark tresses, and gave each of the caterers a smile. "Go ahead and start packing up. As long as they're in disposable containers, I can take the leftovers to one of the nurse's lounges. We'll make sure nothing goes to waste."

The two workers whose names she couldn't remember wasted no time in moving the remaining food from the stainless steel buffet dishes to the aluminum take-home cartons. Within minutes they were wheeling their portable workstation out the door, and Rylie was left to take stock of her kids.

A few had skipped the meal because of nausea from their treatment. One patient — Makayla — had eaten against doctor's advice. She'd paid the price with too much time heaving over the toilet in the small bathroom attached to her room.

Most everyone else was smiling. All in all, the day could be counted a success.

"You ready to go, hon?" Her mom stood still, eyebrow raised.

"I should check on the volunteers at the main unit. They'll be finishing soon."

"I went and peeked in on them." Jessica Durham never ceased to amaze her. "The caterers are breaking everything down, and the others are visiting with the kids. They'll be along shortly."

Rylie glanced at the room to her left. She should leave, but…

"Go ahead. Look in on her. I'll wait."

It wasn't as if she and her mom had any big Thanksgiving plans. With just the two of them, they'd never seen a need to roast a turkey or devil the eggs, but still, they always spent the day together. Usually with club sandwiches, homemade lemonade, and way too many cartons of ice cream, since they could never agree on a flavor. Christmas was much the same.

"I won't be long." Rylie hurried away before she second-guessed the wisdom of her choice. Emotions from the night before were unrelenting and still far too close to the surface. She swallowed them down, though, because one of her kids needed her.

"Hey Rylie." Makayla's tired voice greeted her as she stepped into the room.

"Hey yourself. I hear you overdid it today. Feeling okay?"

"Eh. Been better, but that's how it goes. The drug schedule waits for no man, woman, or child." Sweat beaded on the teen's brow, giving her waxy skin an even greater sheen.

Makayla's parents slipped out of the room, allowing them some privacy.

"So, what made you think today was a good day to go against doctor's orders?"

The teen's eyes darted to the large picture window framing the sky before returning to meet her gaze. "It's dumb."

"Try me."

"What if this was my last Thanksgiving? I wanted to enjoy it."

A fissure ripped through Rylie's heart, but she couldn't let that affect her words. "What if it is your last? What then?"

Makayla tugged at the sheet draped over her legs. "Then I'll spend next Thanksgiving in heaven. I've got that Jesus stuff figured out."

Rylie bit her bottom lip before speaking again. "Was it worth it?"

The teen shook her head. "No, because if I'm not here next year, my parents will be, and their memory of my last Thanksgiving will be of me puking my guts out. It was stupid. I don't care anymore if I die. At least not for me. But Mom and Dad, they're the ones who will have to live with it, you know? I should have thought about them today. Like I said, dumb."

Rylie gave the teen's hand a reassuring squeeze. "It wasn't dumb, and neither are you. Not one bit. You're allowed to think about yourself on occasion. Isn't that supposed to be part of being a teenager?"

A sullen stare met her words.

"Come on. There must be something I can do to help. The holidays are in full swing. What can I do to make this year special for you and your folks?"

A dull spark began to glow in Makayla's eyes. "Anything?"

"You name it."

"I'm finally old enough to go to the winter formal at school, but I'll be in the hospital. This course of treatment..." The teen shook her head. She'd been accepted into a drug trial, an intensive one. The side effects were severe enough that the doctor running the trial had insisted Makayla be hospitalized for the duration — six long months, an eternity to a teenager.

The teen's gaze darted away before returning. "In case… You know, in case this is my last Christmas, I want it to be the best one ever. For my parents' sake. I want them to have pictures of me all dressed up. Maybe even get to dance with my dad. That would make for an awesome Christmas. I'd be okay with it being my last one."

Coming from any other kid, Rylie would assume that mentioning her parents was a ploy to gain sympathy. Cancer kids learned how to work the system, and who could blame them? Makayla, however, was too blunt. Rylie closed her eyes and battled against the torrent of emotion threatening to break free. Keeping a professional distance was always a struggle, but this young woman, the first patient she'd met upon starting her job with Child Life six years prior, had found her way into Rylie's heart without even trying.

Once her emotions were under control — or she could at least fake it — Rylie nodded her head and opened her eyes. "I'll find a way to make it happen."

The toll that chemo and the day had taken on Makayla faded away as eyes previously lit with a small spark now glowed bright. Her smile spread wide, and she threw her arms around Rylie, squeezing her tight. "Thank you."

Rylie hoped beyond hope that she wouldn't let the teen down.

Ten

Black Friday was done and gone. Cyber Monday was upon them.

Rylie would spend her day running from room to room. To account for the reduced Thanksgiving staff, all nonessential tests and scans had been put off until the next week. The result? As usual, the Monday following Thanksgiving was a hospital madhouse.

Rylie hadn't called Zach over the weekend. She'd wanted to, had thought of it at least a dozen times. Sunday's sermon was a mystery to her. Rather than listening, she'd spent the time mulling over whether or not to reach out to the man she was trying not to think about.

He could have made the decision for her by emailing, but he didn't. Her computer remained woefully silent all weekend long.

Did he know she knew?

His niece was the secret he'd been keeping. Rylie had seen too much in her job to take his silence on the subject personally. Everyone handled pain and grief differently. Some people talked. Some refused. Others didn't even know how. And then there were those...

Rylie sighed.

When someone was inherently protective of those they loved, and something came into their world that they couldn't defend against, their whole identity was brought into question. What happened when a protector was robbed of his or her ability to protect? Whether he realized it or not, Zach's actions — and silence — were a subconscious response to his innate need to protect Cassidy. By not giving voice to the threat she faced, he was attempting to keep her safe from it.

It wouldn't make sense to someone who hadn't lived it, but Rylie had seen it before. She understood what he was doing, even if he didn't.

Her mind wouldn't stop circling the subject of Zach York.

She should let it go, let him go. He would reach out when he was ready.

Despite the bucket of cold water that common sense wanted to dump over her head, Rylie couldn't help but feel things for him that didn't make any sense at all, common or otherwise.

They'd shared conversations and emails, enough that she believed she knew who he was. He liked to tease. He cared deeply for others. He was generous and kind. And when something hurt him deeply, he withdrew, preferring silence on the subject.

Rylie wasn't sure it was enough of a foundation to call what they shared a relationship. At the same time, to say it wasn't a relationship felt like a lie.

Between a CT scan for Geoffrey, a newly admitted patient, and an MRI for Giselda, Rylie pulled out her phone. The time had come to stop contemplating and to take action.

"Long time no see. What's up?" Zach's voice came across the line, and Rylie was at a loss. A not-so-secret part of her had hoped for voicemail.

"Uh, hi."

"Hi, yourself. Did you need something?"

She rolled her eyes at her own lack of grace. Good thing this conversation was taking place over the phone. "Listen, I have an idea for December, but it's just for the Oncology unit. Your mom told me about your niece, and I'm not prying, but I need you to know that if this turns out to be too difficult, you can say no, and there won't be any hard feelings."

Silence filled the line.

"Zach?"

He sighed. "Tell me your idea."

Maybe she shouldn't have mentioned his niece. The words had spilled out before she could stop them. "Do you remember Makayla?"

"Teenager, colorful wig."

"Yeah, that's her. That girl's been in and out of the hospital several times. They're battling her third recurrence with her cancer, and she's undergoing an experimental treatment." How much time should she spend softening what she was going to say next? She couldn't see his face. Was this a bad day, or should she just say it? "She's afraid this might be her last Christmas. She'll be in the hospital, too, and won't get to go to her school's Christmas formal. This is the first year she's old enough."

Rylie blinked back the heartache. "I promised her a formal. Fancy dress, decorations, photographer, the whole shebang. She wants to dance with her dad and get her picture taken all dressed up so her parents will have something to... to remember... in case she doesn't make it to another Christmas. I was going to create the dance in her room, but I got to thinking over the weekend. None of us is promised next week, let alone next Christmas, but these kids especially are in danger of not living long enough to enjoy it. How can I not give this gift to them? And their parents and families... Those photos matter so much after a child is gone. If it's in my power to give them some good memories to cherish and some smiling pictures to remind them of those good memories, then I'll do it."

Silence rolled across the line.

A technician waved at Rylie to tell her they were ready to head down for the MRI.

She'd been hoping for too much, pushing too hard. "I should go. One of my kids needs me."

"I'll help." The words were short, his voice gruff. "Let's meet sometime this week and make a game plan."

Rylie stepped toward Giselda. "Montecito's?"

"Sure, but I'm trying the flan this time. I can do tomorrow night or the next. Text me the details."

"Will do."

He hung up before she could say goodbye, but it didn't matter. He planned to help. Rylie's middle hummed with the energy of a high voltage wire. She'd done the right thing. Zach needed this as much as Makayla did. Maybe even more.

Giving her full attention to the young girl in the wheelchair, Rylie put on her brightest smile. "Hey, Giselda. Did anybody tell you what to expect in the MRI?"

The little girl shook her head, eyes wide. Rylie took the girl's hand in her own and gave it a squeeze. "The M stands for Magnetic. Because the machine uses magnets, there can't be any metal in the room when it's running. It's super noisy, too, but that's the worst part. Nobody's going to poke you with a needle or try to draw blood or anything like that. You do have to lie as still as a statue, but…"

"Can you come in with me?" The girl's voice was small.

Rylie gave a brief shake of the head. "I'm afraid not, but I'll be in the next room, and I'll have a microphone so I can speak to you the whole time."

"Can you read me a story?"

"Absolutely. Which one?"

The girl nodded. "Princess Paige and the Band of Purple Pirates. It's by my bed."

Rylie jogged back into the girl's room and grabbed the book before squeezing into the elevator next to the technician and nurse.

Zach arrived ahead of her. Rylie spotted his beat-up truck as she pulled into the packed parking lot. Montecito's was doing healthy business for a Tuesday night. Unless he wore a neon sign, she would need a double dose of luck in order to find him.

In a customarily seat-yourself restaurant, a line of people waited for tables. Rylie turned her head from side to side looking for Zach, but it wasn't until a whistle split the air and drew everyone's eyes to the back corner that she spotted him.

Their waitress outpaced her by seconds, delivering their nachos. Her water-with-lemon sat on a paper coaster at the edge of her place mat. Rylie slid into the booth, her back to the restaurant, and nodded her thanks to Zach. "You remembered," she said, indicating the glass.

"It's not a complicated drink."

She pulled the notebook from her purse and set it on the table.

"Do you mind if we pray first?" Zach's voice rolled across the lacquered wood that separated them, catching her off guard.

"N-no, I don't mind."

He gave his customary shrug. "I was dealing with some stuff, and… Anyway, someone reminded me recently that I shouldn't walk away from something I've been invested in for pretty much my whole life."

Quick to bow her head, Rylie folded her hands and hoped her thoughts stayed hidden. *Thank you God for keeping Your arms open to welcome him back.*

Without fail, whenever she thought she'd realized what God was up to, He flipped everything upside down and sideways. And as was usually the case, the picture He created in the process was stunningly beautiful compared to the one she'd been working on in her own mind.

Zach's voice drifted across the table, deep and solid. "Thank you, God, for bringing my attention to the needs of pediatric hospital patients. I'm sorry it came about this way, but I'm grateful for the opportunity to help. Thank you for all the work Rylie does for those kids to make their lives easier. Please bless this food to our bodies, and help us to plan a Christmas formal that will put the school's to shame. In Jesus' name, Amen."

She smiled. Zach sounded different. Lighter, maybe even happier, but definitely better. She liked it.

"So who should I thank for the reminder you received?"

He stared at her with eyes that reflected hope and helplessness in equal measure. Up to now, his norm had been to reveal as little as possible. Any change in that was an improvement.

Zach blinked, and all traces of the battle waging within vanished. "My niece. She gave me quite a lecture."

"She must be something else. I get the feeling you don't typically take advice from others."

The hint of a smile touched his lips and transformed his face into a thing of rugged beauty. "Are you going to tell me the plan or leave me hanging?" He nodded toward her hand. She gripped her pen in the ready-to-write position. Her notebook was even opened to a page full of notes, but she couldn't recall having turned the pages.

Rylie shook her head to clear it. Important work awaited them, and she couldn't let herself get lost in the fog of uncertain emotion vying for her attention. "We need to find a place willing to rent tuxedos to our boys at no charge and someplace to get formal dresses for the girls. Decorations, too. What about a disco ball or one of those lights that turns everything into a rainbow? Even if I could afford one, there's no room for a disc jockey, so we'll have to figure something else out for music."

The oncology unit was circular in shape with the nurse's station in the middle. The outer ring of the circle held all the patient rooms, as well as the small kitchen, and the utility and supply closets. A small waiting room anchored one end of the circle, but other than that, the floorplan was open. The wide walkway between the nurse's station and the rooms allowed for beds coming and going, as well as foot traffic. Kids walked laps, sometimes accompanied by IV poles. Or if they were younger, they might get pushed by an older sibling or parent in one of the unit's race cars.

Even with the open and inviting space, fitting in sound equipment would be a stretch.

"Are you going to tell the kids ahead of time, or is it going to be a surprise?"

Rylie ran a pen down her notes to remind herself what she'd decided. "We'll tell them in advance. Parents will want to plan to be at the hospital that night and maybe even dress up."

Zach nodded. "Then get song requests from all the kids. Let each one pick a favorite song plus two others. Get me the list, and I'll buy the music — every favorite plus as many of the others as I can. If I load the songs onto my MP3 player and bring it and the docking station plus a few external speakers, it should be good enough. I can check with a party supply place about disco balls or other easy-to-install lighting features. Do you know anyone who rents tuxedoes?"

"No, but one of my kids from this last year has a mom who's a wedding planner. She might be able to help me get that sorted out. I'll call her tomorrow."

"And the dresses? Can girls rent dresses? Tuxes, I understand, but I thought women — or anyone of the female persuasion — wanted to own what they wore."

The man was too adorable for his own good.

"I'm hoping my wedding planner mom can hook me up. A friend of mine dated a soldier. When time came for the Army formal, she wasn't sure yet if the relationship was going to work out, so she rented a dress instead of buying. If Erin, the wedding planner, can't help, I can always ask my friend."

Zach's eyebrows shot up.

It had made sense at the time. Spend three hundred dollars on a dress to keep and wear again, or spend $100 to rent and get the dress, shoes, and matching jewelry. Now that she thought about it, though, the story did kind of make women sound mercenary. Not every woman determined her clothing budget based on how serious she thought her relationship was, but still...

"What are you going to do to thank the companies that help out? All Miguel wanted was for you to include a little sign at each food station saying which restaurant had donated the meal. The people you'll be dealing with this time might want more."

Good point. "Maybe I can print a program? Like an old-fashioned debut or something. Put the kids' names, say 'presented by' and include their parents. Decorate it up fancy and add a page to list everyone who donated something... It could work."

"But what if a new patient comes in that day?"

Rylie bit her lip for a second. "If I design it and type in everyone's information ahead of time, I should be able to print and compile the programs the day of. That'll allow me a chance to make last-minute changes if needed."

"Sounds good. Are you planning to use the hallway as the dance floor?"

She nodded.

"You might want to check the building's fire code."

He was full of sunshiny news today, wasn't he? Without the hallway for dancing, her plan was as solid as Swiss cheese.

Zach cut into her thoughts. "Talk to whoever you need to at the hospital, and if they tell you it's going to be a problem, call the mayor."

Rylie frowned at him. "What can he do?"

He countered her frown with a grin. "In case you didn't hear him any of the dozen times it came up with the kids during the costume contest, the man used to be a firefighter. He's the guy who would know which loopholes to jump through. Who knows? You might be required to have a fire marshal on hand, or additional security, or something. Or you'll have to keep it to no more than twenty people on the dance floor at a time. Regardless, I'd say the mayor is the man to ask if you hit a road block with the hospital."

Somewhere in the organized chaos of their planning, the nachos vanished, their orders were taken, and now their food made its arrival. Rylie's fajitas filled the air with their scrumptious sizzle while Zach's tacos de adobada took an understated approach and offered up a mouth-watering aroma without all the fanfare.

Her first fajita disappeared to the applause of her taste buds before Rylie spoke again. "You might be onto something with the whole mayor thing."

Zach winked at her as he reached for the little bowl of salsa. "Gotta keep coming up with the good ideas so you'll keep me around."

The flutter in her belly was appreciation for the good food. It had to be. His wink couldn't be that powerful... Could it?

leven

Rylie's phone buzzed to life in her pocket. *Zach's here.*

Today was the day. Well, not *the* day, but one of the days.

Zach had connected with Petra Mayhew, a photographer he'd crossed paths with on a residential construction job the previous year. The homeowner had hired her to take before, during, and after shots with the hope of getting their place into some sort of homes-of-the-rich magazine. Petra was donating a day to them and was coming to the hospital to take photos of the kids in all their dance finery. She had already been booked elsewhere for the night of the party, but in the long run, this would work better. Doing the glamour shots ahead of time would mean there wouldn't be a line of dressed-to-the-hilt children waiting to get pictures done while their friends from the unit danced and enjoyed themselves. The photographer was also willing to come back for a makeup session in case anybody wasn't up to having their photo taken today.

With the help of nurses and technicians, the small oncology waiting room had been converted to a studio. If it weren't for the cramped quarters and complete lack of any usable lighting, it would put the finest studio in Northern Virginia to shame. Thank goodness Petra had her own lighting equipment. At her suggestion, though, they'd cleared out the cluttered furniture and draped some neutral material along the back wall. A couple of stools remained nearby so Petra could create different poses as needed. In addition to taking the photos, she planned to provide each family with a digital copy of the three best shots and an eight-by-ten of her personal favorite.

The day flew by, and from formally elegant to slapstick silly, the children made it through their photo sessions. The parents would either be moderately pleased or absolutely thrilled with the results. The day could be marked down as a win.

Thanks to Erin, the wedding planner mom, clothes for the boys and girls were out on a three-day loan agreement so they could accommodate the schedule for photos and the dance.

All eight boys on the unit wore first-rate tuxedos. Erin had contacted a tuxedo shop to which she often referred her grooms. In return for all the past business she'd sent them — and with the hope of future business — they were happy to contribute. The manager of the store had even told Rylie they'd be able to accommodate any last-minute changes or additions that came up. Apparently a group of boys who didn't care whether or not they matched each other was a dream job compared to some of the big weddings and overbearing mamas they often dealt with.

As for the girls — the entire unit had filled with squeals of delight when the dresses had arrived. The company providing them had left them with some extras, too, just in case any new girls were admitted to the unit.

Rylie took a moment to reflect as she checked yet one more item off her to-do list. *Thank you, God. None of this would be possible without You. At every turn, You've put people into my path in order to make this event a success. Again, thank You.*

If Suzie hadn't invited the mayor to participate in the costume contest two months before, Rylie wouldn't have been able to call on him and ask for an introduction to a few willing firefighters. As it turned out, their dance wasn't breaking any official building code. The hospital legal team had been nonetheless reluctant to agree to it. A couple of firefighters volunteering their time to be on site during the festivities had turned out to be the perfect persuasion technique to convince the lawyers to sign off on the dance.

If Zach hadn't sought help from Miguel for Thanksgiving dinner, she wouldn't have known who to ask for donated beverages. Miguel even threw in the fancy fluted plastic drinking glasses she never could have afforded otherwise.

If she hadn't known of a wedding planner mom, she would have been lost when it came to finding tuxedos and dresses for everyone.

If Abigail hadn't mentioned her granddaughter Cassidy, Rylie wouldn't have been aware of a hospital in Japan that housed a young patient Zach cared for so deeply. And she wouldn't have been able to work out the surprise she had in store for him.

Oh, yes. There was no denying God's hand had been in this from the beginning.

The big night, after much anticipation, arrived. The dance was scheduled to start soon.

Thank goodness for the short days of winter. They couldn't keep the kids up too late but wanted it to be dark enough for the disco lights to have an effect. A five o'clock sunset was exactly what the doctor ordered.

Lighting was set on low in each of the patient rooms. Small disco balls hung at intervals around the doughnut-shaped dance floor. Two firemen were stationed at the entrance to the unit. They would make sure the unit didn't go over its capacity and would clear the area should an emergency — medical or otherwise — occur.

The oncologist-on-call arrived clad in a tuxedo. The nurses wore scrubs designed to look like tuxedoes because the evening gown scrubs had all been sold out. The nurses would break the ice and get the party started when it was time. What shy three year old in pig tails would say no to dancing with her favorite nurse, especially when that nurse wore funny tuxedo scrubs?

Parents and teens alike had their cell phones out and in camera mode. The teens had even picked a hashtag to use so Rylie could later track down their pictures on social media.

One of the hospital administrators had pushed for the event to be held in the cafeteria, but Rylie was glad she hadn't been swayed. Nobody wanted to dance with the stale odor of broccoli and fried chicken hanging in the air. Besides, they wouldn't have been allowed to decorate as much down there. It might be a larger space, but it wasn't their space. Most of these kids handled their health with aplomb. For some of them, though, the diagnosis was still new and being away from the relative safety of their hospital room scared them and worried their parents.

She had made a good call by insisting the dance be held on-unit. The smiles on the faces of her kids were well worth the minor bureaucratic scuffle.

A hush fell over the crowd, and Rylie searched to find the cause.

Ah, that explained it.

My word. If Zach had been sexy as a cowboy, he was downright dangerous in a tux. His crisp blond hair was freshly trimmed. Against the backdrop of a black tuxedo, his mocha eyes surveyed her with knee-wobbling intensity.

Rylie hoped he liked her surprise.

She offered a weak smile and stepped over to meet him. "You brought the music?"

He gave her a distracted nod. "Mm-hm."

"You got all their requests?"

"Mm-hm."

"Is everything okay?"

Zach's gaze zeroed in on her with pinpoint focus. Then, as she watched, his eyes changed. Gone were the orbs of burning intensity, and in their place were two pools of molten chocolate.

Oh dear. That man had sex appeal written all over him.

"I like your dress."

Rylie glanced down at the red dress sprinkled with faux crystals. She was, after all, attending a Christmas formal. Red might not be her best color, but it was perfect for tonight. "Thank you." Shyness, something she wasn't used to experiencing, fluttered to life in her belly and robbed her of further words.

A small hand tugged at her dress. "Miss Wylie, are we gonna get stahted soon?" Five-year-old Emma stared up at her with big blue eyes. She'd been a late-in-life surprise to her parents. Her big brother, ten years her senior, was the patient, and Emma adored him. Rylie had caught him glancing toward Makalya's closed door all day long. That's why sweet Emma was asking about getting the dance started. Her big brother had sent her.

A quick glance at the wall clock told her the start time was still a few minutes away. She squatted down in front of Emma and whispered with a smile, "Tell your brother ten more minutes, okay? We're still waiting for a couple of parents, and we need to get the music hooked up."

The girl scampered off, and Rylie craned her neck to see what Zach was doing behind the nurse's station. His hands fiddled with an electronic cube with some other boxy things sitting around it. "So what's our plan?"

He looked at her with the eyes of a man who had much more than mere music on his mind. "Save me a dance?"

"Sure, fine, okay, but that's not what I meant."

It wasn't fair that he could fluster her with a few simple words.

Twelve

The dance was well and truly underway when Rylie brought out her tablet. The gathering resembled a wedding reception more than a high school formal, but she was okay with that. Little kids danced with older siblings, moms danced with sons, and dads with daughters. It was the perfect Christmas formal.

Rylie thumbed through the items on her screen as she looked for her chat application. Over in Japan sat a hospital with a unit full of cancer kids who had never been to any kind of American dance before. After emailing back and forth with the Child Life Specialist there — with help from some online translation software — Rylie had invited them to the party. It was still early morning in Japan, but a dozen kids were up early and crowding around a similar tablet in Cassidy's room.

Delivering the night's program to each of the families was all the excuse she needed to carry her long-distance guests around the dance. She showed them the decorations and captured each of her kids in their evening apparel. Her cancer kids, in on the secret from the beginning, waved and shouted greetings to their counterparts on the other side of the world.

She and her long-distance friends were visiting with a family at the punch bowl as Zach caught up to her. "You taking pictures with that thing?" He pointed toward the tablet in her hands.

"Uh, you could say that."

"Hi Uncle Zach!" Cassidy's voice was almost lost in the noise of the party surrounding them, but recognition dawned on his face before her words faded away.

Without asking, he took the tablet from Rylie's hand.

"Isn't this great, Uncle Zach? Miss Rylie contacted our hospital and invited us to your dance. Nobody here's ever been to an American dance before." The girls around her all chattered in rapid-fire Japanese. Cassidy rolled her eyes. "Akiko says you're a... a beefcake. Cho says she'd ask you to dance if we weren't, you know, thousands of miles away."

Zach's eyes bore into Rylie before he returned his attention to the screen and smiled at his niece. "Why wasn't I aware of this until now?"

"I asked Miss Rylie to keep it a secret. I wanted to surprise you. I'm, you know, proud of the stuff you've been doing there. Take it from me — anybody who takes time to make life better for hospital kids is a superhero."

Tears misted Zach's eyes, but he blinked them back. "You want to dance, Sweet Pea?"

"Okay, but then you have to promise me you'll dance with Miss Rylie. She's smokin' hot in that dress. She should be dancing more than she has been."

Zach lifted his eyes. His words were directed at his niece, but his eyes remained on Rylie the entire time he said them. "Either you need glasses, or we have a bad connection. Smokin' hot doesn't do her justice. Not at all."

Then, a thoughtful smile on his face, he took the tablet out to the floor and shared a dance with his niece. It was awkward and beautiful, peculiar and perfect. And precisely what Rylie had hoped to give him tonight. A special memory with the girl who meant enough to him that he had willingly stepped into the unknown world of pediatric illness and injury. Even as Makayla wanted this one special night because she wasn't sure she'd live to experience another Christmas, Rylie wanted to give this gift to Zach... *just in case.*

The song came to a close too soon, and he returned to Rylie's side in time for Cassidy's words to reach her. "Go dance with her already!"

He looked from his niece to Rylie before answering. "If I dance with her, what am I supposed to do with you?"

A nearby nurse snatched the tablet out of Zach's hands. "Got you covered. We'll watch the whole thing from over here."

Zach led her out to the oddly shaped dance floor with the eyes of his niece and every cancer kid in the unit on them. Some of the boys gave Zach a thumbs-up. The girls soaked in the scene with dreamy eyes, some of them no doubt imagining what their first grown-up dance would be like someday.

They didn't get more than four beats into the song when all the little eyes around them faded away. Rylie's world grew smaller and smaller until all that remained were her and the man who held her in his arms.

She'd anticipated the warmth of his hand against her back. The electricity, however, was unexpected. It shouldn't have been, but it was. Currents originated where his hand met her back and sizzled along every nerve ending in her body. All the time she had poured into preparing this event for the kids, and it hadn't occurred to her that she needed to prepare herself.

Zach was hurting. He fell into Rylie's life because he was brokenhearted over Cassidy's illness. Just because she felt more alive in his arms than any other time in her life didn't mean anything. He was dancing with her to please his niece, not because he...

"That dress is breathtaking on you. But then, you're stunning in jeans, too. And scrubs. I never thought of scrubs as sexy until I saw them on you." His lips brushed against her ear, and this time the simple sizzle of electricity graduated to a full-fledged lightning bolt that robbed her of the ability to breathe.

Zach pulled back and searched her eyes. "You're a beautiful person, Rylie Durham. Inside and out, forward and backward… I'm sorry it's taken me such a long time to say so. I felt guilty for being attracted to you. I felt guilty for finding joy in your presence when Cassidy was so sick. I know she's my niece and not my child, but still. I felt…"

She couldn't pull her eyes away from the mesmerizing movement of his lips as she waited for his next words.

"I never expected to have kids of my own, you know? My sister married young, started a family, and then discovered along the way that she would only be blessed with one child. I, on the other hand, never married. I'd kind of accepted that being an uncle was as close as I'd get to fatherhood, and it's a role I'm honored to fill. Then you came along, and suddenly Cassidy's health wasn't the only thing on my mind, and I felt guilty for that."

Zach continued to hold her close, his voice low enough that it wouldn't carry beyond the circle of his arms. "I wasn't entirely on speaking terms with God there for a little while, but as soon as I started talking to Him again, He reminded me that guilt isn't mine to give. Making myself feel badly over good things happening in my life doesn't do my niece any good." He gave his trademark shrug then, and Rylie couldn't help but revel in the sensation of his muscles flexing under her left hand.

They were still on the dance floor, but their movements had slowed to more of a sway than anything else. They could have been the only ones out there for all the notice Rylie gave the other dancers.

"And I'm one of those good things?"

A mischievous grin shaped Zach's mouth. "Sweetheart, you are a master of understatement."

Rylie bit her bottom lip, fighting the urge to smile back at him.

"You either have to tell me you feel the same way or tell me to get lost, but you can't leave me hanging. It's dance protocol."

"Dance protocol, huh?"

He nodded sagely.

Rylie leaned up on her toes as she tugged his head closer to her own. Whispering against his ear, she told him, "I happen to think you're a good thing, too. In fact…"

The song came to an end. Into the silence, a voice yelled out from the other side of the world, "Kiss her, Uncle Zach!"

He tipped her chin up with a single finger, a tiny touch with the power of an intimate caress. His lips met hers then, warm and enticing, firm yet gentle. He tasted of lemonade, sweet and tart like she'd imagined.

The kiss was over too soon. He pulled away to the sound of applause and catcalls erupting around them.

A grin teased the corner of his mouth. "In fact?"

Rylie resisted the urge to touch her fingers to his lips. "In fact, I can't think of a finer thing that's come my way in a long time."

His eyes crinkled at the corners as his teeth flashed white. "Does this mean I can take you out to dinner sometime, and we can talk about something besides the hospital?"

Rylie tossed a coy smile his way as she took his arm. "It means you had better."

Zach led her back to the nurse's station. He reached for the tablet and told his niece, "You sure are good at stirring up trouble, aren't you?"

The girl giggled.

"We need to wrap things up here. Is it okay if I call you in the morning? Later tonight your time, before lights-out."

"I'll be waiting," she chirped back at him. "I figured out what you should do in January for the hospital. I have an idea about Valentine's Day, too."

Zach blew Cassidy a kiss as Rylie waved to her and the connection was severed. "Thank you for letting her be a part of this. I know she's not one of yours."

"By the looks on the faces of her friends there, they all enjoyed the chance to participate in an American dance, untraditional as it may have been."

He shook his head doubtfully. "They might have enjoyed the dance, but the thing they're going to be telling everyone about is the kiss. Go ahead. Try to deny it."

"Yeah…" Dread pooled in Rylie's belly.

Zach's eyebrow lifted. "What?"

"If word gets back to the hospital administration, I might get in trouble for that one."

"Don't you worry about a thing." He clapped his hands and gained everyone's attention. In a loud voice, he called out, "I'm not naming any names, but somebody hung mistletoe in several places. I suggest you look up and see if you need to take action."

The entire unit broke out into celebration as everyone began moving around the circular dance floor going from one person to another and kissing them on the cheek. A few of the kids made gagging noises as their parents kissed each other — not on the cheek — while others chanted, "Kiss, kiss, kiss."

Zach leaned close, his words a warm tickle against her skin. "I'm pretty sure you can't get singled out now."

hirteen

Three days had passed since the Christmas formal in Oncology. The twenty-fifth was still two days away, and the entire unit — which still buzzed with excitement over the dance —looked forward to celebrating.

"Social media exploded with pictures of the dance." Rylie got the words out between bites of salad.

Zach's eyebrow lifted. "Exploded?"

She grinned. "I'm simply repeating what I was told. Glad to know I'm not alone in feeling outdated."

Rylie was hampered with an upcoming late meeting at the hospital. Escape wasn't possible, but Zach had wanted to see her, so they were sharing dinner in the cafeteria. The salad was good and all, but Montecito's would have been better.

Who was she kidding? Anytime with him was good.

"In case I haven't already said it, thank you for making Cassidy a part of the dance. My sister and her husband say the same." His voice moved from husky to hoarse.

He'd said it. Several times. "You want to talk about it?"

"I can't, not without wanting to put my fist through a wall. Or maybe cry. I get the two confused."

Rylie glanced up from the greens piled inside her eco-friendly container. "Well, I'm glad your surly mood when we first met had a reason. Not glad for the reason, but…" Words were easier to come by with kids. "Even so, it doesn't mean you don't still occasionally need to talk."

The irony wasn't lost on her. Zach might have been taciturn, but she'd been the surly one when they'd met. Who would have thought then that they would both come as far as they had?

Zach glanced away before picking up the previous conversation. "Cassidy is her own kind of sun. She can't walk into a room without lighting it up. I'm a better person for having her in my life."

Rylie nodded. "Tell me something you guys used to do together before she moved."

He rolled his eyes. "I babysat a lot. I learned the names of all her stuffed animals and even sat through princess movies with her. That was bad enough, but then one time she asked me to paint her nails."

She chuckled. "What'd you tell her?"

"There's a reason I'm not a housepainter. I build things and let other people paint them."

"How'd that go over?"

Heather Gray

His grin was contagious. "She batted her eyes and said please."

"Ha! You never stood a chance, did you?"

"Not even half a chance."

Rylie pushed the remnants of her salad aside and reached for her water. "So, did you become a good painter?"

"Eventually. Every time I babysat after that, she brought out her mom's entire collection of polish. One time she insisted I paint each nail a different color. I told her nothing would match, and she told me I needed more imagination because, with her nails painted that way, she would match everything."

"Let me guess. She had a plan to grow your imagination."

Zach shrugged, but red infused his neck. "She wanted me to let her paint my nails."

Rylie choked on her water. "Oh, dear. And did you?"

The color climbed higher as he mumbled something.

"What was that? I couldn't hear you."

He rolled his eyes. "My toes. I let her paint my toenails. Although she got as much polish on my toes as she did the nails. She wasn't very old then."

"I'll bet she was delighted."

Zach's smile came easy. "It was a long time ago, but I can't bring it up without her laughing hysterically."

Rylie understood better than most. "That's the story you take out and dust off on the days when she's struggling the most."

He nodded and glanced away again. "What if I never get a chance to make more memories with her?"

She reached across the table and gripped his hand. There was a lot she could say, but telling him he would have eternity to make memories once he was with her again in heaven wouldn't help, not right then. So she held his hand. He didn't need answers. He needed to know he wasn't alone and that she was a safe place to share his emotions.

The sound of a vibrating pager broke into their silence. Hers, of course. People in the real world used cell phones, but in the hospital, staff still carried pagers. A quick glance showed her the *911*. She scrolled through the rest of the message as she jumped up from the table.

"I have to go."

Worry etched lines around Zach's eyes. "Is everything okay?"

"One of my kids collapsed." Rylie started to run out of the cafeteria, then stopped. Her kids needed her, but they weren't the only ones. She returned to the table. "Are you going to be all right?"

He grabbed her hand, pulled her back into the booth beside him, kissed her on the corner of her mouth, and then released her. "I'm fine. Go take care of your kid."

Rylie raced into the oncology unit. "What's going on?"

One of the nurses waved her down. "Makayla collapsed. The oncologist's been called to do an assessment."

"Is she okay?"

"Banged her head. She needs a couple of stitches."

Rylie took a deep breath. "Her parents?"

The nurse frowned. "Dad's been notified. Mom was in the room. She saw Makayla start to go down but couldn't get to her in time."

"Was she complaining about not being well? Was there any indication of a problem?"

"You know Makayla. Unless she's in the act of vomiting — which is rare as it is — if you ask her how she's doing, she's always going to say she's fine."

Yeah, Rylie knew her. If ever a girl was too grown up for her age, Makayla was. Cancer did that to kids. Everything became relative, and, "How are you feeling?" was interpreted in terms of how the child had felt during his or her last chemo treatment or following the last surgery.

Rylie dried her sweaty palms on her scrubs and approached Makayla's room. She poked her head around the door. "Hey there. Are you taking visitors?"

The teen beckoned her from the bed. "Come on in. Join the circus." Mrs. Maskey hovered nearby, wringing her hands. A wound care specialist stood on one side of the bed examining the teen's visible bruises. Depending on the type of cancer and the treatment, patients bruised easily, and simple bruises could quickly turn into DTI's — deep tissue injuries. From the other side of the bed, another nurse stitched up a cut on Makayla's forehead.

Rylie grimaced. "The forehead? You couldn't fall somewhere with soft fatty tissue to cushion things?"

Makayla chuckled, and the nurse doing the stitching warned her to hold still.

"You mean I could have avoided all this fuss by falling on my butt? How bad is it?"

Rylie downplayed the knot on the teen's forehead. "Not quite as bad as those old cartoons where someone would get hit in the head and a ten-inch bump would grow from the spot."

"Mom's kind of freaked out."

The teen glanced over at her mother, who raised her arms in surrender. "Guilty as charged."

Rylie shrugged. "Moms are allowed to freak out now and then. Freaking out is in the official mom handbook. They're legally required to do it at least once per month, but they're given leeway for up to once each day."

Makayla rolled her eyes. "I'm fine, honest. I think Mom screamed, though, so some of the others might be worried. You should go make sure everyone else is okay." The teen wasn't saying the words, but the message was loud and clear. *I don't want to talk about it in front of Mom.*

Rylie stepped toward the door. "I'll do that, but don't be surprised if kids pop in all evening to check on you."

The teen made a brushing motion with her hands, and Rylie allowed herself to be swept out of the room.

The meeting was over, and exhaustion tugged at Rylie's shoulders. She'd been asked to serve on a hospital committee whose purpose was to determine the necessity of different programs and services available to the pediatric patients. She hated it. Cutting the pediatric budget seemed to be the committee's entire goal. Every meeting turned into a battle. Wait until one of those committee members had a kid in the hospital with a deadly illness. Then they'd understand. Until then...

Rylie sighed.

She wouldn't wish a deadly illness on anybody — child or adult — but still. If those people got out of their offices and bothered to go down to the units they complained about, they'd appreciate how every penny was spent. They would realize how important it was for kids to have toys to play with and movies to watch. If they ever sat in with a family receiving a terminal diagnosis for one of its members, they'd understand the importance of having chaplains available. If they bothered to go to the MRI suite when a terrified and hysterical child was told to lay still for an hour-long MRI, they would see first-hand how vital Child Life was.

Those problems, unfortunately, would still be there tomorrow. They could wait. Makayla couldn't.

The unit was quiet. Most of the parents had gone home for the night. Some of the kids were asleep. Others stared at the TVs in their rooms.

She made her way to the teen's room. The lights were out, but the glow from the hallway caught the flash of her open eyes.

"Hey. Is it okay if I come in?"

Makayla gave her a tired smile. "Sure."

Rylie slipped quietly into the room but didn't turn on the lights. After a hit on the head, her eyes might be sensitive. Then again, maybe she didn't want anybody to be able to read her face and thoughts.

"Want to talk?"

Makayla shrugged.

Rylie sat on the edge of the bed. "Do they know yet what happened?"

"Doc says I fainted. They're running a million tests." The teen's voice was dejected.

"Tests are nothing new. Why so down this time?"

"Stupid doc opened his big mouth and said they were talking about releasing me but wouldn't be able to now."

Ouch. Having the prize within reach then seeing it snatched away... That was brutal.

"I thought the trial forced you to stay in the hospital for the duration."

Makayla growled before answering. "The doc in charge of the whole trial made me go into the hospital because my white count was going wonky. That, and I kept getting fevers. He said he wanted more control over my environment. He's in Chicago, but he let me pick a hospital close to home."

None of these details were new to Rylie, but she let the teen talk.

"Apparently I've been so stinking stable lately that he was talking to the oncologists here about letting me go home for Christmas. Nobody told me in case it fell through. Until that jerk opened his mouth tonight."

The doctor wasn't a jerk, and mentioning Christmas was a mistake he would never make again. Makayla didn't need to hear that, though. She would figure it out for herself in time. She might even feel guilty for calling the guy a name.

The teen spoke into the darkness. "Maybe I was right."

"About what?"

Makayla sighed. "This is going to be my last Christmas, isn't it?"

Rylie scooted closer and pulled the teen into her arms. Tears soon soaked the short sleeve of her top, but she didn't say anything, at least not to Makayla. That didn't, however, stop her from talking to God.

It's not fair. She's spent most of her life in the hospital, and she deserves to go home to be with her family. Give me the words, Lord. Help me know what to say.

No words came, but peace settled across Rylie's heart. She stayed in place and held Makayla as the torrent of tears continued.

Fourteen

"Are you up yet, hon?"

The voice reached through Rylie's fitful slumber and tugged at the edges of her attention.

"Come on, sleepyhead. You told me to wake you."

Rylie rolled over on the couch and stared up at her mom through a cascade of sleep-mussed black hair. The lights of the Christmas tree twinkled to her left as the sun, visible through the living room window to her right, worked its way up into the sky. "Is it morning so soon?" As if the sunlight didn't give it away.

Her mom held out a cup to her, and the smell of coffee tickled her nose and tempted her stomach. Rylie pulled herself up and tucked her feet beneath her on the couch.

Spending Christmas Eve night at her mom's had been a tradition ever since she'd gotten her first job after college and moved out. She reached for the cup and sniffed the air again. Cinnamon, brown sugar, and yeast. *Ahhh.* Monkey bread, another family tradition.

"Merry Christmas, sweetheart. What time do you need to go?"

Rylie rubbed a hand over her eyes and fought to focus. She hadn't slept well since Makayla's collapse, and the whole waking-up nonsense got harder with each passing morning.

With a familiar shake of the head, her mom slipped from the room. The sound of the oven door being opened reached Rylie. The time had come to get moving. She set her coffee on the couch's side table and trudged to the bathroom.

Fifteen minutes later, Rylie returned to the living room. Her face was washed, her teeth brushed, her hair combed, and she was dressed. As for being awake? She needed to drink more coffee first.

Her mug, however, was no longer where she'd left it. Mom at work, no doubt.

Rylie reached the kitchen and the small two-person table tucked away in a corner. The missing coffee sat next to the platter of monkey bread with her mom's cup of hot tea on the other side.

Once she took her seat, Mom grasped her hands and prayed. "Dear Lord, thank You forever for the precious gift of Your Son. We ask You to bless us today, and to help us keep our focus on Christ's birth and, ultimately, on His sacrificial death. Encourage us at every turn, Lord. Lift our hearts and challenge us to wholly seek You. Be with Makayla today as she gets this news. Comfort her heart, be with her family, give them strength, show them Your Love. Hold them tenderly and please, please, please... Please let the test results be good."

Rylie echoed the soft *Amen* and opened her eyes to be greeted by her mom's watery smile. Mom had taught her from a young age not merely to act compassionate toward others, but rather to make compassion a part of her existence in the same way that eating, sleeping, and breathing were. The tears were expected. Anything less, and it wouldn't have been her mom there with her.

"So did they give you any indication of the results?"

Rylie shook her head in answer. "They usually do, though."

"And that has you worried?" Mom nudged the platter of monkey bread closer to Rylie's side of the table.

"I don't understand the timing. They wouldn't deliver bad news on Christmas, would they?"

She'd received a text late the night before. Makayla and her family would be getting the test results this morning.

Oncology rarely saw surprises. Cancer was, after all, usually a slow disease. Most procedures and tests were scheduled during normal business hours. For that reason, only one Child Life Specialist worked the unit — her. When a situation developed outside her schedule, the nurses took care of it and either texted her about it or informed her the next time she came in.

This was Makayla, though.

And it was Christmas Day.

No Child Life Specialists were due at the hospital. All the units were quiet. Every child who could be discharged had been, and nothing of import was scheduled. That's why the text from last night was such a mystery. The oncologist on call for the holiday had texted to inform her he expected the last of Makayla's tests back by early morning and planned to meet with the family between nine and ten.

Rylie couldn't let the Maskeys go through this without support. Granted, everyone on the nursing staff loved them and would do whatever they could to help. But again — it was Makayla, a girl who statistically shouldn't have lived to see her tenth birthday because of her first cancer and who had nonetheless survived two recurrences since. A girl who, at age sixteen, put on a positive face for her parents not to escape their hovering, but rather to give them good memories of her. A girl who... a girl who had stolen Rylie's heart six years earlier when they'd first met and whose every stay in the hospital since had been an exercise in joy and torment.

She had to go. She wasn't sure she'd be able to forgive herself if Makayla needed her and she wasn't there.

"Are you going to take even a single bite?"

Rylie peered from her still-empty plate to her mom's sad eyes. "I want to throw up."

A nod met her words. "I had to try. You go. Be there for that girl, and love her and her family the best way you know how. I'll still be here when you're done."

"I don't want to ruin your Christmas."

Mom began fitting plastic wrap over the untouched monkey bread. "We all have good days and bad, Ryles. It's nobody's fault if a bad one falls on a holiday. The only thing that will ruin my Christmas is if you don't come back here and share your day — whatever it turns out to be — with me."

Rylie headed for the front door and put her jacket on. Winter had finally shown itself with the fury of a wild beast in Northern Virginia, so she reached for her scarf, too. A quick jog back into the kitchen brought her to her mom's place at the sink where she was washing out their cups. "Love you, Mom." She gave the woman a tight hug before heading back to the door.

"Love you more, my pretty."

The words floated behind her. The *my pretty* was an inside joke so old neither she nor her mom remembered how it had started, but still, it was comfortable and familiar, and on a day like today, those things mattered.

What would Makayla be facing? Bad news had become far too familiar in her short life, but it would never be comfortable.

FIFTEEN

"I can't begin until…" The oncologist's words trailed off as Rylie entered the room.

Were they waiting for her? She wasn't that important.

The oncologist gave Rylie a grateful look. "I was explaining to the Maskey family that we need one more person, then we can get started."

Makayla offered a wan smile before her eyes shifted to the door and dread filled them.

"Ah, Doctor Pratt, it's good to see you." Relief flowed through the oncologist's voice like water through the crack in a dam — natural and forced at the same time.

Rylie took in the new addition. Dr. Pratt. She'd never met him. He was the head researcher for the drug trial. He had been to visit Makayla twice — once before she started the drug trial and then again when he made the choice to hospitalize her for the duration of the treatment.

His presence sent Rylie's stomach on a roller coaster ride hurtling through the darkness.

Doctors didn't travel across the country on Christmas Day to deliver good news. Then again, decent human beings didn't travel across the country on Christmas Day to deliver bad news.

By the look on the faces of Makayla and her parents, they agreed.

Doctor Pratt strode into the room, grabbed a chair from its resting place against a nearby wall, flipped it around backward, and straddled it. He folded his arms across the top of the backrest. "My natural mode of communication is science. I want to explain what's going on with your treatment, but if I get too sciency, feel free to jump in, okay?"

Not a *hello*, or a *how've-you-been*. Straight to business. Being a research doctor must void the need for a bedside manner.

The visiting doctor's entire focus was on Makayla, and as soon as she nodded, he began. "I was in the midst of studying the cellular response to various chemo drugs when I noticed a correlation between mitochondrial reactions, the replication of certain amino acids, and the behavior of human t-cells…"

Makayla cut him off. "The science stuff is interesting and all, but are you here to give me good news or bad?"

"Good, I think."

"Good for me, or good for future generations?"

"Both, I believe."

Makayla sucked in an audible lungful of air, a stunned look on her face. She smiled at her parents, who had been still as statues since Dr. Pratt's entrance. They'd stood there holding hands as if their lives — or their daughter's life — depended on it. They both started to rush toward the bed then stopped themselves. They retreated and sank onto the room's wide window seat instead.

Rylie could only guess at what they were going through. Good news, after all, was relative. Did good news mean a cure? Or one more year? Both were good, but they were very different types of good.

Dr. Pratt's eyes wandered the room until he met Rylie's gaze. "Child Life?"

"Rylie." She held out her hand with a nod.

He shook it. "I'm not good at the people stuff, and I know it. I visit a different hospital almost every week as part of this drug trial, and I can't tell you how grateful I am for all the Child Life Specialists who spend their days making up for the shortcomings of doctors such as myself." Then he winced. "I mean, relationship shortcomings, not medical."

Rylie couldn't help but chuckle. "You don't say." She waved her hand toward the hospital bed. "I think you can get back to your sciency stuff now."

Dr. Pratt swung back to Makayla and gave her a wide smile. "Shall I continue, or do you want me to fast forward?"

Her eyes sparkling, the teen told him to pick up where he'd left off.

A thirty-minute lecture about the cellular effects of cancer drugs commenced. Dr. Pratt explained why his drug was different and how he hoped it would revolutionize pediatric cancer treatment in America. If it proved itself in this trial, he believed the methodology would be applicable to other cancers as well.

By the time he took a breath, Rylie was ready to sign up for his drug trial, and she didn't even have cancer, let alone the specific one he was going after. Nor was she anywhere near his targeted age group.

"Is the drug actually doing what you designed it to?" The question came from Mr. Maskey.

Dr. Pratt pulled off a nod-shrug that gave nothing away until he spoke. "Of those who have finished the treatment, we've seen an eighty percent remission rate. We don't know yet how long the remission will last, but early signs indicate a positive outcome for patients."

Eighty percent... *Wow*. Eighty percent was unheard of with Makayla's cancer.

"Am I... Am I in remission?" The teen's breathless question, wrought with hope, pulled on every single one of Rylie's heartstrings.

Dr. Pratt nodded. "We need to finish out the treatment, but as of your last scans and blood draw, you appear to be cancer free."

"Why did she collapse?" Mrs. Maskey's voice cut through the room, a razor-sharp blade that demanded attention and allowed no celebration. They'd had remissions before, and they'd lost them.

The doctor hung his head for a moment before answering. "Every drug comes with side effects. This one appears to impact the pancreas in about fifteen percent of participants. The pancreas produces the insulin that..."

"Has the pancreatic side effect been fatal to anyone?" Mr. Maskey ignored the brief glare from his wife.

Dr. Pratt nodded, reluctance etched into the lines around his mouth. "Twice. I take responsibility for not stressing more thoroughly the importance of frequent blood sugar checks. Had more diligence been exercised in checking and documenting their levels, we might have caught the problem sooner and been able to get proper treatment for them both."

He'd taken the blame rather than saying it was the kids' fault for not checking their sugar levels more often. In a world where malpractice seemed to lurk behind every corner and medical professionals had gotten so used to avoiding blame that excuses were more common than platitudes, his approach was refreshing.

Still, Rylie wanted to read those two files. She'd ask him later. Now wasn't the time. After all, it was Christmas.

Rylie stepped into the hallway and collected the balloons she'd left there out of sight. She brought the enormous bouquet of red and green balloons into the room. Every crevice, crook, and cranny of her car had been crammed, trunk included. Stepping close to the bed after depositing the gift, she grabbed Makayla's hand. "Do you need anything?"

The teen's grin lit up the room. "I'm good. Really good. Thank you for coming in."

"Anytime." Rylie squeezed her hand then waved to Mr. and Mrs. Maskey, who continued to ask Dr. Pratt questions.

Rylie made her way to the elevator and down to the ground level. She walked across to the parking garage and paid little attention to her surroundings until her car came into view.

"Hey." Zach leaned against her sedan, a cup of coffee in his hands.

"Isn't it a little cold out here?"

He reached onto the roof of her car and retrieved a second cup, holding it out to her. Rylie opened the driver's side door and stowed her purse behind the seat before taking the proffered drink. She closed the car's door and leaned back into the cold metal, inches from her dancing cowboy philanthropist.

"What brings you to the hospital on Christmas Day? Doesn't your family have some big tradition?" In truth, she hadn't asked about his Christmas plans. She'd just assumed.

"We're celebrating tonight so we can video chat with Cassidy and her folks."

"How's she doing?"

His look was thoughtful as he gazed into the distance. "The doctors are optimistic, which is new. I'm taking it as a good thing."

Rylie nodded. A doctor's attitude could change an entire family's outlook. "So you never did answer me. What brings you to the hospital?"

"I tracked down your mom, and she told me where to find you. She invited me to join you for turkey sandwiches and ice cream but said I'd have to stop by the store and get my own. She wasn't sure if she had my kind."

Rylie laughed. She'd seen the freezer. It held no less than eight different flavors. "What's your poison?"

"Vanilla."

Heaven help them. "Looks like we'll be stopping at the store then." He'd picked the one flavor neither she nor her mom ever bought.

"Works for me."

"We do an informal Christmas." Rylie had never made apologies for the way she and her mom celebrated the holiday, but she wondered if their tradition would appear lacking to Zach. "We read the second chapter of Luke, and we each share a special way that Christ's birth has impacted us in the past year. We don't have a fancy meal or do gifts, though. Time together is our gift to each other. That's always been…"

How was she supposed to explain it? At one point, all her mom could afford to give her was time. Then, when she eventually got to a place in life where she could give more, time was all Rylie wanted or needed.

Rylie started to push herself away from the car, but he stopped her. He took the coffee from her hands and set it, along with his, on the roof of her car. Then he reached for her, turned her to more fully face him, and pulled her in.

Zach's hands rested at the base of her back. He held her loosely, but the look in his eyes was far from casual.

"How is Makayla?"

Her smile came, and the joy in her heart bubbled up and spilled over into a single word. "Remission."

His brow furrowed. "Her collapse?"

"Blood sugar, a side effect of her treatment."

Zach tilted his head back and sighed. He looked at her again, the shadows gone from his eyes. "I'm glad. I was worried for her. For you, too, and how you would take the news if it was bad."

Rylie shrugged. "Some days my job is harder than I ever imaged it could be. Those days leave me exhausted and in tears. Other days leave me angry and asking God what He's doing. Most days, though... Most days are rewarding and filled with joy."

"You fill my days with joy."

She didn't bother fighting the silly grin playing tug-of-war with her lips. "Do I now?"

Zach pulled her closer. "Tell me I'm not in this alone."

Rylie reached up and rested her hands on his shoulders. "You are most definitely not alone."

"You don't make anything easy, do you?"

What could she say? Tell him she enjoyed the chase? That flirting with him was more fun than she'd had in ages? She stretched up on her tiptoes and whispered against his lips. "Not if I can help it." Then she touched her lips to his in what was supposed to be a quick kiss.

He took over, though, giving her the most thorough kiss she'd experienced in her life. Blood rushed through her veins as his hunger threatened to consume her. Then, without warning, he broke away and pulled back.

His bottomless eyes held her pinned in place, preventing her from looking away. "I'm falling in love with you, Rylie Durham."

The feeling was mutual, but she'd rather kiss than talk. Common sense prevailed, though, and she opted to lighten the mood. Passionate kissing in a secluded and dimly lit parking garage wasn't on her top ten list of Wise Choices to Make in December. "So... vanilla, huh? We need to work on that."

He blinked several times as her words — or lack thereof — registered.

She smoothed the collar of his jacket and rested her hands on his chest. "I'm not sure I can love a guy who prefers vanilla ice cream over all the other options out there."

Understanding dawned, and his eyes came alive. "Hm," he said, capturing her hands in his. "Maybe you'll have to convince me to find a new favorite." He brought her hands to his mouth and brushed his lips against the backs of her fingers before releasing them and opening the car door for her. "I'll follow you."

Rylie pulled into the parking lot at her mom's apartment complex. Festive lights twinkled in various windows.

Zach brought his truck to a stop next to her and climbed down, grocery bag in hand, and opened her door for her. "Before we go in, I'd like to tell you what Christmas means to me this year. I know I might have to say it again at lunch, but I want you to understand first."

Rylie shut her car door. "You have my undivided attention."

He shifted the bag from one hand to another. Twice. Then he started to talk. "I was reminded this year that Jesus came and lived a life here on earth, fully man and fully God. I don't entirely understand what that means, but I get the *fully man* part. He faced the same struggles as me. So when life gets hard, and I don't like where it's going, I can take it to Him, and He understands. I don't have to hide from Him when I'm hurting or doubting. For me, this year, celebrating Christmas is about remembering that Jesus gets me. Loving people comes with a cost, but He's not callous to that cost. He met people and loved people and experienced grief. I know Christmas is the celebration of Jesus' birth, but this year has taught me that it's also a celebration of His life. It's because of His life as a man that I can draw close to Him, that I can let Him walk beside me. If it weren't for that, He'd be some far off distant God that I couldn't relate to. So…" His words faltered.

"So Christmas is a celebration of life and relationship with Jesus."

Zach nodded. "Exactly."

Rylie reached over and took his free hand in her own. "I like that."

His smile came easier these days. It looked more at home on his face, too. Still… "What's that smile for?"

He lifted an eyebrow. "I'm hungry, and my ice cream is melting."

The man was incorrigible. If anything, his ice cream was more frozen now than it had been in the grocery store. The warmth of her mom's apartment beckoned.

Rylie winked at him and took off at a full run for her mom's door.

He gave chase, his laughter echoing in the cold Christmas air.

The End

Enjoy a peek at Informal Romance Book 2.

AN INFORMAL ARRANGEMENT

Chapter One

"No, no, *don't flush the toilet!*"

Maddie ran into the room, assessed the situation, and placed her hand on the patient's shoulder, shaking him lightly. "Mr. Jenkins. Mr. Jenkins, it's just a dream." This was her first day working with him, but he'd been on the unit for a while. Nothing in his file indicated a history of night terrors or bad dreams.

The man in the bed groaned and thrashed. "Not... albino... horned toa'... Please, no." Was he talking about toes or — a shudder tore through her — toads?

Had he seen one? She fought a shiver as she searched the immediate vicinity. No toads — horned or otherwise — in sight. He was obviously dreaming, but still... What did a horned toad look like, anyway? Not a frog with antlers, surely.

Every off-white nook and cream-colored cranny of the room came under careful scrutiny as Maddie continued speaking to her distressed patient. "Mr. Jenkins, wake up. You're having a nightmare."

His eyelids fluttered for a moment before opening. When he saw her, Mr. Jenkins' eyes grew wide. A remnant of sleep slowed his voice. "Is everything okay?"

What was she supposed to say to that? Tell the poor man he'd awakened her deep-seated dislike of all creatures not cute and furry? Or worse, explain how that dislike had been birthed?

"You, uh, were having a dream." Brilliant response.

"I was?" He scratched along his stubble-darkened jaw, emanating a masculinity that belied the days he'd spent in the ICU. "I kind of remember it. Was I talking in my sleep? I do that sometimes." He glanced around and licked his lips before whispering, "Is there a reason you seem so alarmed?" His voice, smooth like hot apple cider on a cold winter's day, warmed her.

Maddie blinked. She shouldn't have let her mind go down that path. Some thoughts didn't belong at work. "You mentioned something about a toad…" Her remark hung between them like a two-day old helium balloon.

The worry wrinkles on his forehead faded away, melting into his hairline and drawing her eyes to light chestnut hair that couldn't seem to make up its mind whether it wanted to stand at attention or lie down and take a nap.

"Umm, I guess I remember. Huh. I wonder where that dream came from." If his nonchalance was anything to go by, he had to dream about toads on a regular basis.

"And you mentioned the toilet." Maddie took a deep breath and went about her morning routine. Shift had just started, and she still needed to do her patient assessment.

She put the blood pressure cuff on Mr. Jenkins as he told her about his dream. "There was an albino horned toad that got out of its terrarium. It was in the toilet for some reason, but because the commode was white, nobody could see it. Which doesn't make sense. Albino animals aren't pure white, but what can I say? A hand reached for the lever to flush, and I panicked. That's when you woke me."

After she charted his blood pressure and listened to his heart and lungs, she asked, "What exactly is a horned toad? I'm picturing something froggish."

Mr. Jenkins laughed, disturbing Maddie's attempt to count his pulse. He reined himself in, and she began counting again. "Frogs and toads are different, you know, and a horned toad isn't even a toad. Not really, anyway. It's a lizard."

Her eyes darted around the room again. Maddie worked with people — and not animals — for a reason. "So toads and frogs are different, but a horned toad isn't a toad."

"That's right. The people who discovered and named it must have been confused."

Maddie held up an index finger. "Hold on a second." Then she marched over to the small attached bathroom. An empty toilet had never been so beautiful. She stepped back into the room. "Whew. All clear."

When her patient chuckled, she knew she'd hit the mark.

"Are you sure you're not the one who's confused? A toad that's not a toad?" She quirked her eyebrow as laughter sparkled in Mr. Jenkins' eyes.

"I'm never going to live this down, am I?"

"Are you aware you've been the talk of this unit?" Maddie kept up the banter as she continued her assessment.

"We're in the ICU. Being talked about might not be such a good thing." The strain of his current health situation didn't bleed into his congenial voice.

Some patients were better than others at compartmentalizing. They put their problems aside, lived in the moment, and in some cases wouldn't even acknowledge whatever illness, predicament, or condition had landed them in the hospital. Maddie often associated such behavior with men, but Mr. Jenkins was taking it to a new level. She decided to prod. "You're improving more rapidly than anyone here expected. We're all happy for you."

"I didn't do anything. All the credit goes to God." As if an afterthought, he added, "And the medical staff here, of course."

Maddie turned away. It wasn't his testosterone-dominated brain at work. Faith was to blame. Her stomach lurched. "So if it's not a frog or a toad, what is it?"

Mr. Jenkins graciously allowed the change in subject even though he'd already told her once. "A lizard. The cool thing about it is how, when it feels threatened, blood shoots out of its eyes."

Maddie made the mistake of trying to picture a blood-shooting lizard atrocity. She didn't get far in her attempt before dots danced in front of her eyes and she realized her mistake.

Poor Mr. Jenkins shot a look at the monitors that showed the readings from the various pieces of medical equipment attached to him. Obviously she hadn't kept her reaction from showing. His eyebrows drew together as he studied the data. A second later, he lifted his hands, palms out. "You're, uh, losing color. It's not as bad as all that... Is it?"

Blood shooting out of eyes wasn't bad? Nothing in his chart indicated early-onset dementia. Perhaps she should review the list of medications he was on.

"You'll likely never come across one around here, anyway." His placating voice asked forgiveness while his confused eyes said he didn't know what he'd done wrong. "They're mostly in the southwest."

"Mr. Jenkins, how are you doing today?" Dr. Sage stood in the doorway, his tall form and imposing physique a contrast to the patient in the bed.

"Good, thank you. Please call me Holden." His eyes shifted to Maddie. "You, too."

"Of course," the doctor replied before turning to her. "How are his vitals?"

"Steady," she told him. "Heart rate was elevated, but he'd just woken from a dream. It quickly came back down to normal."

Dr. Sage raised both eyebrows. "I do believe, Holden, that patients all the way over in the next wing are now afraid to flush."

Color crept up his neck and into his cheeks. "Was I that loud?"

"Not at all." The doctor's tone was drier than the Sahara during drought season.

Holden winced.

A chuckle softened the stern lines of the doctor's face. "But you did add a little spice to our shift change this morning. To be honest, if a patient is going to yell at the top of his lungs about something, I'd much rather it be the toilet than the care he's receiving."

Holden shook his head. "You've all been great. Having said that, I can't wait to get out of here, and I hope I never meet any of you again. At least, not under these circumstances. No offense intended."

"None taken." The doctor tipped his head to the side. "On that note, I've got some news. We'll be transferring you out of the ICU later today to a bed on the main floor. You've got a long recovery ahead of you, but you're no longer in imminent danger."

"Do you know yet what caused all of this?" Holden waved a hand to indicate his body.

The doctor frowned. "There are still several tests pending. At present all we can say for certain is that you presented here at the hospital with Transverse Myelitis, apparently subacute. You didn't suffer a stroke or obvious spinal injury, and we could find no tumor, slipped disc, or other abnormalities to indicate the cause of your problem."

Holden wanted to know what had put him in the hospital. Maddie was pretty sure he didn't want a list of everything that hadn't landed him in their care.

The doctor cleared his throat. "Sorry. We're a teaching hospital. Sometimes I forget to take the teacher hat off." With a shake of the head, he began again. "We're still considering a viral cause. Have you heard of viral meningitis?"

Color drained from Holden's face as he nodded. "Is that different from transverse…?"

Dr. Sage held up a hand. "Sorry. You don't have viral meningitis. It's just an example of how perfectly ordinary viruses, when they get into the wrong places in our body, can cause devastating damage."

"So I got a virus?"

The doctor's head bobbled back and forth for a second before he answered. "The problem for us is that, while there are a few main culprits when it comes to Transverse Myelitis, the sheer number of known viruses makes it challenging to pin down the cause. We're also running genetic tests to look for certain markers that might help us pinpoint underlying causes. It may be several weeks before we have a definitive answer."

"What sorts of underlying causes?"

Maddie gritted her teeth. Sometimes less information was better for the patient's peace of mind.

"I'd rather not worry you until we know something." The doctor studied Holden for a beat before continuing. "And I have to be honest. We might never know. Test results aren't always clear-cut."

Holden opened his mouth, but before he could speak, the doctor's pager went off. He glanced at the device and read the screen before shaking his head. "I have to run. Maddie can answer some of your questions, or your doctor when you get out on the floor. If I don't see you again before then, I wish you all the best." The doctor held out his hand, and the two shook.

Dr. Sage rushed from the room and Maddie was left staring at a none-too-happy patient.

"Is it always this hard to get answers?"

Tact could be overrated. This wasn't one of those times. "Sometimes we run tests for diseases that would terrify most people. If we're checking you for every imaginable horrifying illness known to man, do you really want to know that?"

"I have a right to know."

"Of course you do, but you weren't entirely coherent when most of these tests were ordered. Dr. Sage wasn't trying to hide anything from you. That's not the kind of doctor he is. He probably just didn't know how to answer the depth and breadth of what we've looked at so far."

"Can you give me an overview?"

"Sure. You're in your early thirties, so most of the age-related causes are off the table. You don't have HIV or systemic lupus erythematosus. We found no evidence of varicella zoster, herpes simplex, hepatitis, or rubella. They haven't ruled out Devic's disease or multiple sclerosis as underlying causes yet, and some of the virus tests are still outstanding."

He ran a hand down his face.

"Do you want me to stop?"

Holden nodded. "I think I've heard enough for now. What happens if they can't narrow down the cause?"

Maddie offered a half-shrug. "Your official diagnosis would become Idiopathic Transverse Myelitis. Idiopathic just means the cause couldn't be identified."

One of the other nurses stuck her head into the room. "Maddie, they're waiting on you to give report on your patient in 203."

"I'll be right there."

She turned back to Holden, who waved her off. "Go ahead. I'm fine."

With her thoughts moving ahead to her other patient, Maddie gave him a distracted nod. "I'll be back in a little bit to get breakfast ordered and take care of anything else you need."

She heard his soft "Thank you," as she slipped out the door.

When Maddie walked back into his room, Holden's eyes were closed. Curtainless windows framed the tips of bare trees. January in northern Virginia was stark, grey, and frigid.

She stepped closer to the bed to check on her patient, trying not to wake him if he was sleeping. As she leaned in, his eyes popped open, and she jumped. Her reaction had little to do with his sudden movement, though. In truth, the crisp emerald green of his eyes caused her unexpected response. How had she not noticed their gem quality earlier? Oh, that's right. She'd been too busy checking the room for reptiles. In the intensive care unit, no less.

"I'm sorry," he said. "Did I startle you?"

"Your eyes are the same color as a frog." Maddie fought the urge to grimace. Holden would have every right to regale the floor nurses with tales of his frog-toad-lizard obsessed ICU nurse.

He didn't, however, take advantage of the chance to mock her. "I get the feeling you don't much care for them."

A shudder moved up her spine and shook her shoulders. "I'm not fond of any animal without fur on at least some part of its body." How did they keep ending up on this topic? Maddie needed to change the subject, and she reached for the first question that came to mind. "What would you like for breakfast? Anything in particular?" Hopefully she could prove there was more to her than a phobia he likely thought silly. Not that his opinion mattered. She wouldn't see him again after he left the unit.

"Bacon."

His gusto tugged a reluctant smile from her. "Once you're out on the floor, you won't get to order your meals whenever you want. You'll need to submit your requests a day in advance, and you won't have as many choices. So let's make the most of your last day in intensive care."

She skimmed the menu before picking up the phone and calling down to the kitchen. "This is Maddie. I'm the nurse for the patient in room 723, Mr. Jenkins. I'm calling to order his meal."

"Mr. Jenkins, room 723... All right, go ahead with your order."

"He would like the bacon breakfast burrito, with pork bacon instead of turkey. And the bacon breakfast sandwich, also with pork bacon, but without the egg, cheese, or English muffin, please. Orange juice to drink and..." Tossing a saucy grin at Holden, she said, "You know what? Go ahead and add a side of bacon to that. Pork, though. Not turkey."

The man taking the order sputtered for a bit before asking her to hold. A supervisor's authorization was required before the order-taker could approve such a gluttonous combination. The kitchen was supposed to serve healthy meals. Go figure. The bacon-fest of an order she'd placed jeered at such constraints.

Maddie whispered to Holden, "You'd never be able to do this, but I might get away with it." She gave him a playful wink as the order-taker came back on the line and rattled something off. "Yes, I understand, but we need to get some calories into him. He's lost a lot of weight." The gentleman again consulted someone else before coming back on the line.

The phone wasn't even back in its cradle before Holden, eyes filled with glee, asked, "Well?" His body practically vibrated with eager curiosity as his hands clutched his blanket and he leaned forward in bed.

Laughter tap-danced along Maddie's skin and through her voice. "They asked if you'd like bacon ice cream with your meal. It's something new they decided to try, but apparently none of the patients will eat the stuff."

He looked like he'd just taken a swig of curdled milk.

"Is that the face I made when you talked about that critter shooting blood out its eyes?" Moving to his bed and dropping the side rail, Maddie said, "Okay, let's get you over to the bathroom. I'm assuming you need to go, but if you don't, you can at least brush your teeth and splash some water on your face. That ought to feel good after so many days in this bed." Maddie began disconnecting the various monitors attached to her patient.

Holden glanced from her to the lavatory and then back at her. "Were you planning to come in with me?"

Maddie had witnessed many different reactions over the years, but Holden's blushing uncertainty pulled on her heart strings. "First things first. Let's get there. Then you can tell me if you think you're able to manage on your own."

189

Mutiny swept briefly across his face.

"You're still in the ICU, Mr. Jenkins, and you're in my care. I won't take chances with you. Let's see how steady you are on your feet by the time we've made it to the bathroom. Then we can argue if you want."

Holden swung his legs down over the side of the bed, and with her support slid off the edge of the mattress, planting his stocking-clad feet on the floor. They were hospital issue stockings, too, complete with non-skid bottoms, one-size-fits-all shapelessness, and a must-have-been-on-clearance nauseating green color. He swayed back and forth before getting a handle on the appendages once again doing their job of supporting him.

"We can take our time. No rush." Maddie had been briefed. She knew the history of his illness. Holden had brushed it off, assuming it would pass. Until his legs had begun to fail. He'd taken his symptoms seriously then. By the time he could get an appointment with his personal physician, though, his mobility had further deteriorated. The culprit was most likely a virus, but with the way it had ravaged his body, it was a miracle Holden stood at all.

"Do you want the walker?"

He eyed the folded-up item leaning against the far corner of the room.

"No." His answer came through gritted teeth. Holden's progress across the room was slow, but he

Author's Note

Thank you for taking the time to read *An Informal Christmas*. I want to take a quick minute to acknowledge the hard work that goes into caring for pediatric patients. I would also like to say that not all hospital administrations are as uncaring as painted in this story. Rylie needed some conflict in her work life, and as I plotted out the story, it became apparent that the hospital administration would have to be the culprit.

If you would like to support a children's hospital in your area, I encourage you to get in touch with their Child Life department and find out what they need. If you don't have a hospital nearby or don't have time to shop for and deliver items, then please consider giving to an organization that raises money to provide toys and encouragement for hospitalized children.

About the Author

Heather Gray writes inspirational romance, including the Ladies of Larkspur western series, the Regency Refuge series, and a handful of contemporary titles.

Heather loves coffee, God, her family, and laughter – not necessarily in that order! She writes approachable characters who, through the highs and lows of life, find a way to love God, embrace each day, and laugh out loud right along with her. And, yeah, her books almost always have someone who's a coffee addict. Some things just can't be helped.

Despite being born into different eras, Heather's characters share a common trait. They're all *flawed...but loved anyway.*

You can find Heather online and sign up for her newsletter at www.heathergraywriting.com.

Other Books by Heather Gray

Informal Romance (Contemporary Christian Romance
An Informal Christmas
An Informal Arrangement
An Informal Introduction (May 2016)

Ladies of Larkspur (Inspirational Western Romance)
Mail Order Man
Just Dessert
Redemption

Regency Refuge (Inspirational Regency Romance)
His Saving Grace
Jackal
Queen

Contemporary Stand-Alone Inspirational Romance
Ten Million Reasons
Nowhere for Christmas

made each step under his own steam. A safety harness was in place around his waist, and Maddie had a hand on it in case he needed help, but he never faltered.

By the time they got to the bathroom door, beads of sweat shone across his brow. The question wouldn't be welcome, but it needed to be asked. "How do you feel? Will you be okay in there on your own?"

"I'll be fine." The reply was short, but not unkind.

She offered him a reassuring smile. "Let me give you a hand over the threshold. There's a little step up there, and I don't want you to trip. Then I'll leave you to see to matters. You've even earned yourself a closed door. I'm going to be right here outside the door, though, so if you run into any trouble at all, speak up."

An inscrutable expression met her words.

"Don't let embarrassment get in the way. If you need help, ask. This is my job, not just something I do for jollies. Besides, it can't be any worse than asking for help with a bedpan."

As soon as the door closed, Maddie swept a hand across her face. She wouldn't be surprised if he locked the door. *For jollies?* Where had that unfortunate phrase come from?